FUNEREAL DISEASES OF THE MIND

Fifteen tales of dark erotica

 Published in the United States by Hexed Flesh Books, a division of Krysalgen Publishing, Gaithersburg, MD, USA.

ISBN 978-0-578-02212-3

To my parents,
Without whose love I wouldn't be half what I am,

And to my wife,
Whose love completes what my parents began.

<u>TABLE OF CONTENTS</u>

FIDEM MEAM NOTO
(See How I Am Faithful)

The rains were beginning again.

Rain made it perfect.

He'd chosen the Sumatran ceremonial mat, circa 1870, for tonight's proceedings. Past civilizations had treated textiles of its sort as precious gifts from deities of their day. Articles such as this one were only brought into usage on the most auspicious occasions—often as rarely as four times in a century. Tonight's circumstance seemed as appropriate.

Gurhan bent over Priestess Damiana where she lay upon the mat-draped bed to place a kiss upon her forehead. Scalding tears threatened to overflow his eyelids but he held these back as he always did, because his tears saddened her. Tonight was their anniversary. Nothing could be allowed to disrupt their celebratory mood.

His lips came away from his wife's forehead bespeckled with mucoid flakes of her flesh. Her unseeing spoiled-milk eyes wept ichor like rancid wine, like maniac mascara, staring up at nothing, observing everything.

Outside, the infidels were re-grouping, organizing another assault on the temple; biding their time. Gurhan sensed them out there even before the priestess alerted him to their presence, fouling the night like leprous shadows laying their sinister plans against Damiana. It was his job to sense such developments. Gurhan hefted the ceremonial artifact that would protect her from those who would see her brought low. It felt as right and perfect in his hands as Damiana herself once had.

“My sacred priestess,” he whispered into what little straw-like hair remained rooted to the mottled gelatin scalp. Bouquets of rotted-away crimson hair lay strewn about the pillows. Those brittle curls retained their luster, even now. Cheekbones like tent poles split the drawn flesh of her face.

The voice of his priestess sounded within Gurhan’s head, whispered into his mind.

Where. . .are my faithful? she asked, *Cold. . .so cold. . .Where are my paramours? Fetch my playthings for me. . .*

“Of course. I’ll collect them at once,” he told Damiana’s corpse, “The best of your selected faithful. The ones you’ve chosen.” Gurhan left his queen, returning momentarily with three visitors come calling.

Beyond the ancient temple’s stones, the night screamed for the souls of the unworthy. Lightning scorched the sky, making of the night air a fire in which Gurhan could feel himself burning.

At Gurhan’s direction, the visitors removed their shrouded tunics. Damiana’s worshippers tonight were two priapic gods of alabaster and mahogany, and a Bedouin with features and curves so Junoesque that kingdoms of a bygone era would have warred over her mystique. Tonight her name was “Roshni.” The two males, Gurhan had christened “Dalin” and “Kho.” They stood naked and humbled, letting their Thai silk garments whisper to the floor.

Need. . .Give them to me, Damiana demanded, *Body needs release. . . tongues. . .Give me them quickly. . .*

“Holy one,” Gurhan announced reverently to his departed love, taking his place at her feet, “Greater love hath none than these who stand before you now. They come to worship you as the embodiment of sensuality.”

Bloated maggots burst from a wound in one of her upraised knees. They crowded between her blackened toes, slid from her ears sporadically, dropping onto the pillow beneath her head with sickening sounds.

"Money cannot buy the honor bestowed upon you this night," Gurhan advised the visitors, "Let your tributes reflect that knowledge." He wielded the ceremonial artifact, caressed its metal hide as one would a cherished partner. The visitors took their places upon the ceremonial mat. The time had arrived for them to express gratitude for their spared lives.

Worm larvae scrambled from the putrescent chasm of Damiana's throat to burrow into her split lips. Roshni brushed these away and mashed her mouth against that scabrous wound. Her lush raspberry-painted mouth dragged away bits of Damiana's lips like fraying parchment. Tears stung the sultry woman's eyes, meandered down her cheeks to salt her lips and Damiana's.

From the darkness beyond the windows, night winds blustered their approval. Roshni closed mournful eyes and sucked at the slick lips. A spiral of her kohl-black hair fell across Damiana's face, collecting slime as it dragged the corpse's eyes. Voyeuristic storm winds gusted again, flaunting their libidinous might. Thunder thrummed through the room like a lover's moan.

Damiana's voice resonated again within Gurhan's head. *So warm, their mouths*, she told him, *So warm and wet. . .as wet as I'll be for all but you, because you were never worthy. . .*

"Please don't, Priestess," Gurhan whimpered, watching Roshni nibble the spoiled meat of Damiana's forearm, watching Kho's taut shoulders flex as he bowed between her holy thighs to rim her navel.

Tongues fucking me. . .fucking the way you never could. . .

"I loved you. I *loved* you. Please don't say such things," Gurhan pleaded. His grip on the ceremonial artifact blanched his knuckles.

Lightning ripped the clouds. The percussion of rain against windowpanes crescendoed as Dalin chewed the rotting digits of her left foot. Maggots clung to his lips as if demanding their measure of his love. Smearing his chin with the vile soup of her decay, he pushed his tongue between rigored toes, tasted green, noxious flesh. He licked slimy threads of putrescence from his lips before continuing to plant kisses along her calf, moving toward her face.

These sensations. . . the priestess quavered inside Gurhan's head, *so loving. . .How naïve of me, taking a eunuch for a lifemate. . .*

Gurhan's face and hands began to burn the way they always did when his priestess cuckolded him. Tonight reminded Gurhan of nights when she was still alive, and his place in her house was on his knees.

The lapping affection of Kho's tongue set her sacred vagina oozing. Gurhan watched the necrotic flesh swell, smelled the fetid syrup of her arousal. He watched its lips strive for lush pinkness even as the rest of her body lay rotting. The shriveled black pustules of her nipples approached firmness under the siege of Roshni's teeth and Kho's tongue and Dalin's fingers. The priestess grew wetter still as fevered hands assaulted her liquefying breasts, as adoring tongues searched her rotten mouth, tasted the fungus colonized between her fingers.

"Now," Gurhan huffed, nestling the ceremonial artifact against the back of Dalin's head as if in coronation, "Do it now!" Reverent tears washed Dalin's face as the sinewy brown worshipper took his place between the thighs of the priestess. Reaching between the younger man's thighs, Gurhan hefted his dangling fruit, guiding it toward Damiana's blossoming labia.

Dalin's girth sank slowly, splitting her ripening vagina under Gurhan's direction. Inordinate tightness, a sort that remained a rarity in any living woman, greeted Dalin's stroke. Sinking himself in the dead woman to the hilt, he pulled back his rancid-smelling stiffness before thrusting it forward again hard. And again. And yet again.

Delicious. . . Damiana gushed, sounding euphoric.

From beyond the bedroom door, a muffled clatter sounded; the bravado of conspirators who had run out of patience for subtlety. Frantic footfalls. Cries of hate drawing nearer from the corridor. Panic like a frigid, twisting blade speared Gurhan's stomach. His temple had been breached. The infidels were inside.

"Priestess!" he started. The cacophony of splintering wood and busting lock mechanisms pre-empted his warning. Another blow from the unbelievers' battering ram, and the bedroom door exploded inward.

How *dare* they desecrate his temple, his priestess in such fashion, thought Gurhan.

The infidels storming the seventeenth-century mansion came in full riot gear. These were no local sheriffs. They weren't Feds. These men were something else entirely, something far darker than even the most covert of black-ops units. Apparently, the reputation of Gurhan's Cherrywood Farm and Winery was growing. He forced an inviting smile for the helmeted men rushing into his bedroom.

"Freeze! Everybody on the ground! Now!" they barked.

"Jesus tap-dancin' Christ, what the hell is that stink?"

"Don't you move, mister! Hands! Show me your hands! NOW!"

Damiana's three worshippers seized the confusion of this interruption to dive from the bed, abandoning their priestess in favor of begging the officers, "Waste the motherfucker! Blow him away!" Roshni scrambled into a corner of the room, where she would sit hugging her knees until the officers physically removed her. It was survival instinct alone that up until now had guided her ability to force action from her limbs. Now that Gurhan's power to coerce had been compromised, she wasn't moving a fucking muscle and nobody would make her. Not ever again.

To the officers attempting to soothe her, she could only say, "He should die for the things he made us do. . .sickening, terrible things!"

"What in God's name was he doing in here, Sir?" a young latte-skinned officer asked the commander of the operation, a shaven-scalped mammoth of an entity who wore no nametag, but whom Gurhan knew simply as "Ridgefield." The younger man, whose armored black uniform identified him as "Lawson," eyed the three abductees. He could almost hear Kho's silent prayer for Gurhan to give these intruders a reason; just one reason to aim one of their semi-automatics at his goddamned throat and squeeze a hot one through his skull.

"What he was doing, Mister Lawson," Ridgefield replied, "was abducting young people who wander onto the property late at night, bringing them here, and forcing them to 'make love' to his dead wife." No one braided fact and fiction so convincingly as Ridgefield.

"I take it this is his wife?" Lawson said, nodding solemnly toward Damiana.

"Nope," came the reply, "His wife's been dead for sixteen years. This is one of the latest harvests from the cadaver farm he keeps hidden beneath the slaughterhouse on the hill."

The younger man's eyebrows leapt. "You can't be serious, sir!"

"As serious as the half-dozen sidearms currently aimed at his head."

"Then the stories are *true*? Never knew the cadaver farm was real. I've known about the local myths since I was twelve, but. . ." he let his words trail off, shaking his head in disbelief. Tonight, more than ten years since he'd last heard the urban legend, Lawson found that the memory of his older brother's tales when they were teens skipping stones across still ponds could still elicit shudders from him. "Criminology students from the university go there and stake rotting corpses out to finish decaying in open air," Jeremy used to swear to him with eyes big as saucers, "Then they study the progress of the maggots that go to work on the stiffs. They say it takes about two weeks for the little buggers to strip a stiff down to the bare bones. . ."

Sometimes, Lawson would go home and wet his bed at night after they'd talked about it. And tonight, here he stood. Living the nightmare.

Ridgefield went on, "Perfect site for such an operation. Slaughterhouse is *supposed* to smell like death, so no one's the wiser if they should catch the scent of decay."

"Kill him! You have to stop him!" Dalin pleaded, keeping his head covered with his hands even after seeing Gurhan's wrists cuffed securely behind him. Gurhan's beloved ceremonial artifact lie at Lawson's feet and the soldier picked it up, cracked it open, and emptied the shells from it. He handed the sawn-off shotgun to Ridgefield.

"Sir, you'd better come see this," called another heavily armored officer stationed outside the room.

"Christ, what now?"

"More hostages in the upstairs rooms, sir."

"Fucking hell. All right. You handle it. I'll be there in a minute. Mister Lawson, go with him, would you?"

Lawson left. The naked hostages, whose names most decidedly were *not* Dalin, Roshni, and Kho, allowed officers to accompany them into waiting police vehicles where matted fire blankets would seem like Chinese silk shrouds and tepid coffee would taste like love poured into Styrofoam cups. Ridgefield dragged Gurhan into the chair from which he'd watched all the evening's activities.

"Your cadets were almost ten minutes early this time," Gurhan said, "You really must consider having the occasional team of seasoned agents accompany you on these fictitious raids. At least *they'd* know a thing or two about punctuality. But then, anyone other than the neophytes you pluck from each of your organization's graduating classes would see through us both in a heartbeat. Am I right?"

"Quiet," Ridgefield barked at the smaller, older man. He allowed the briefest pause before adding, "You'll remember our deal?"

"Of course," Gurhan smiled. He was almost as fond of his arrangement with Ridgefield as he was of pretending his deceased Damiana was a High Priestess of antiquity, rather than the diseased, adultering dominatrix he'd discovered her to be within the first six months of their marriage.

On some days, the disease she'd given him hurt him worse than on others, but some pains, one simply had to learn to live with. Ridgefield was one such pain, but their arrangement was a good one: in exchange for Ridgefield's orchestrating regular delivery of drugged subjects ranging from runaways to known drug pushers and murder suspects, and Gurhan's freedom to conduct his depravities as he saw fit, one videotaped copy of each evening's events was all Ridgefield would ever require.

"Good. Make sure you do." He released Gurhan from the handcuffs, mere stage props utilized for the benefit of the three abductees that two of his men, posing as local officers, had delivered to Gurhan's door.

In a moment, Ridgefield would join his soldiers, including the two phony cops, to be credited with collaring the three drug pushers just removed from Gurhan's home. He'd stride outside to the phony police vehicles and the abductees therein, apprehended on narcotics possession. There, he'd have one more attempt at persuading them to name the source of the illegal substances they peddled. Should they remain as uncooperative as they were several hours before, Ridgefield would take deadpan glee in threatening them with swift redelivery to Gurhan's secluded compound for an encore audience with Priestess Damiana. Judging by their state, they were going to sing like fucking canaries though, and this disappointed him somewhat. Ridgefield enjoyed fulfilling threats of that nature.

"That wife of yours," Ridgefield said softly, "To go through as much as you go through, actually taking time to. . .You must really hate that bitch, huh? For giving you. . .what she gave you."

Gurhan grinned. "On the contrary, Commissioner Ridgefield, I love her to death." He tried not to laugh after delivering that sentiment, but failed to suppress a chuckle.

Sometime after Ridgefield and his men left, Damiana's voice rose in his mind. Gurhan welcomed it as always.

. . .It appears you really do love me. Perhaps some night soon, I'll allow you to join in the frivolity enjoyed by those whom you

bring to worship me. For now, rest assured that while they may taste my body, you alone have my heart. . .

Greater love had no husband, and Damiana knew it as well as Gurhan did. Who except the man who loved her beyond measure could have the stomach for such affairs as this? He knew not one man who, in his place, would have honored his herpetic priestess's dying request: to be broken by the lusting faithful, embodying carnality to the very last. Lovingly fucked to dust.

That request, the corpse's first, had come sixteen years ago, moments after he'd murdered her. It was the first time Damiana's voice had ever risen inside his head, and damnable shame that it was, the fact remained that Gurhan loved her, even if he no longer *liked* her. That love, like fuel, would keep him at his tasks until his final breath, constantly seeking out new avatars to represent her, new worshippers to appreciate her, or his eventual capture. And Gurhan entertained no delusions of never being caught. Sooner or later, Ridgefield would tire of him and the infidels would come for him in earnest. Whenever they finally did take him, many would call him insane. A monster. A sociopath. But who among them had ever loved as he had?

Gurhan knelt at the priestess's bedside and watched her nipples shrink as the magic fled her dying flesh. He watched the pink glisten flee her sex as the labia returned to their former state of blackened death. In a few nights, Ridgefield would deliver a new wave of worshippers, Gurhan would select a new avatar from his cadaver farm, and the games would begin again. Gurhan smiled at the thought of yet another opportunity to improve his standing in her sightless eyes. He was not crazy. He was not a monster. The way he saw it, Gurhan was merely a desperate husband in love, and Damiana, his cherished bride. For better or for worse.

THICKER THAN WATER

It wasn't lovemaking, the time that Hank and Angela spent naked together. Love had little, if anything, to do with the force of Hank's thrusts, the covetous way he handled her breasts, left them slippery with spit. Love held scant significance to the earnest rollercoaster she carried between her thighs, the way she always swallowed when his orgasm poured him into her mouth. As for things of their collaborative making, the word "love" was about as far removed from their feverish pressings as a word could be.

Tonight, as their twice-weekly ritual had established, they were hooking up at his camper, in his bed. They were screwing as they'd been doing for the past seven months; him filling her with his hate, her engraving disloyalty and ownership across his tumescence. Him throwing himself after her, into her like a suicidal cliffdiver, pushing his malice deep into her chest, a scabrous seed secreted beneath the freshly-turned earth of her nakedness. Her responding with teeth, a sentient cyclone of hair and sweaty epithets spinning away his cares and responsibilities. Her fingernails autographed his sticky back as their pelvises ground his marriage into dust.

His loving and dutiful wife, her responsible big sister, would soon return home from that place out by the airport where she'd been spending two nights a week for too damned long. She would return to their fucked-up little desert camper at the edge of the interstate offramp, smelling of perspiration and dirty cash and other men's lust. She would kiss him hello and tell him how much money she'd made tonight as if all was right and well with world and marriage, but her eyes would not join in the denial that her tone wove into the air between them. Then she and her baby sis would begin World War III over which of them had eaten the last English muffin out of the pantry or left a dirty saucer in the kitchenette's sink, or smoked more cigarettes out of the packs of one-twenties they shared.

He would listen and burn inside to reveal his part in the increasing tension between the sisters. He would consider suggesting that a good threesome might be all they needed to bring the ladies eye-to-eye on things, then decide as always that so much more amusement value lie in the consideration than in the suggestion.

This, at least, was how things would have gone down, had tonight been an ordinary night like all preceding nights had been. But tonight was something else. Tonight signified their last screw, and they'd planned a grand conclusion for their circus of flesh and hatred; a big finish designed to punctuate to Mera the error of her ways, her failings both as a wife and as a sister.

"She's fucking somebody," he hissed, seizing Angela's ankles like Ducati handlebars and making a wish as he drew them widely apart, "You know she's fucking somebody down at that place. Why else would she be hitting the jogging track out behind the high school every morning? She's getting in shape for somebody, and it sure as hell ain't me."

Like the much-missed Ducati he'd sold as one of many marital concessions made over the past three years, Angela could go from zero to sixty in the blink of an eye under a skillful hand. The journey was always well worth the taking. On nights like tonight, he could almost thank Mera for making him get rid of the motorcycle. As far as the ability to handle a rough ride went, Angela beat hell out of the machine. Hank leaned into his act of burying his rigid cock between her thighs and held it there, fell forward to smear his stickiness into hers. Angela crossed her ankles over his ass and sank press-on fingernails into his beefy shoulders.

She bit his earlobe and whispered, "When we were kids, she once locked me out of our house during a freak summer hailstorm so that she could nap without me bothering her. Bitch. I never bothered her."

Hank stabbed himself into Angela with the sort of petulant vigor displayed by a child poking a wounded animal with a stick. Her vaginal clasp tightened on his member, responding as much in reply to his mashing as to their commiseration over Mera's shortcomings. No utterance of verbal filth held more power to roughen Hank's handling or get Angela's arousal flowing than such discourses. Angela snatched the base of Hank skull and hurled her pelvis up to swallow his offering, and up to slap her pussy against his crotch, and up to give back a slamming fuck as primal and as strenuous as the one she lay taking.

"I get so sick of her giving me that 'I don't know if I came or not' bullshit after I've been up in her," Hank growled, wiping his mouth across her taut right nipple before sucking it between his teeth.

Angela gasped, her back rising into an arc that offered her C-cups toward the stars, "Like if she had, she'd have to wonder. Stupid ass." The arm that she locked across the back of his neck headlocked Hank, ground his stubbly face hard against her breast.

"Luckily, it don't run in the family," Hank replied, claiming a handful of her hair and yanking in that way that made her wettest. Hank licked her exposed throat like a gourmand stealing a sample of some exotic dessert. The sound that Angela let out as his teeth replaced his tongue where her shoulder joined her neck, a cry caught halfway between a plea and a demand, drew his scrotum taut. Hank swore loudly, signifying that his time was nearly upon him.

Shuddering, he yanked himself free, heralding his arrival, preparing to anoint Angela's tits and stomach with pearls. She didn't need his verbal warning. She could read the onrushing orgasm in his eyes. Angela held his gaze, shook her head "no," and rolled away from Hank.

There was a certain look that Angela could summon to her eyes, that of an empress deigning to address a beggar, that always drove Hank wild. He knew as well as anyone that Angela's interests in him went no deeper than the joyful spite that she derived from fucking her sister's husband. He knew a guy like him would never in life get a woman like her naked without some monetary exchange taking place beforehand, and that he certainly would not be wearing her juices this moment, had chance placed his wedding ring on any other finger than Mera's. Women didn't exactly climb over one another to bed guys that stood five-foot nine in workboots and carried forty excess pounds around their middles. But rather than intimidating him, that knowledge fueled Hank. Knowing that despite his not being much to look at, he had at least one thing going for him that made him worth fucking well and often, excited him like nothing ever had. Combined with the message unspoken in her eyes, it made an absolute animal of him. That look of amused condescension was present in Angela's eyes now.

"Not there," Angela rasped, rolling onto her stomach, "In my ass. Come in my ass."

"Whore," Hank grunted, chuckling as he took his place behind her, his hands clapping onto her hips like a trap snatching hold of prey. The smell of her sex was opiate. A bead of Hank's saliva splashed onto his belly.

"Lucky you," she replied, reaching beneath the mattress for tonight's big finish while Hank snapped his hips forward and gave the lady what she wanted. Angela came shrieking things that she never had for any other man except her sister's husband.

"Yeah, honey, that's right. Big finish. Big fucking finish!" Hank groaned as he emptied into her. At length, he collapsed beside her, sour with sweat, and as without breath as he was without remorse. Hank reached beneath his side of the mattress and drew out the shiny weapon that he and Angela had agreed upon for him. Hank, unwilling to abide a life wherein his wife's nudity belonged not to him, but to the highest bidder, was about to finish big. She'd be sorry.

"Yeah," Angela rasped, unwilling to be her sister's burden any longer, "Big fucking finish!" Mera would regret making her feel like a dependent.

Angela straddled her brother-in-law's waning cock and buried the serrated steak knife in Hank's throat. The hole that she opened whistled, gurgling and sputtering as he screamed, as she pressed the weapon to its splitting wooden hilt with something like love, but sleeker and oilier, behind her eyes.

Hank squeezed the nickel-plated Colt's trigger and pumped a hot one into her forehead, splattering red-gray rage all over the ceiling above the bed.

Angela's last thought before Hank's bullet punched a moon roof in her skull was that Mera was going to be pissed at her for finishing the last of the milk and replacing the emptied container in the refrigerator.

*****

Mera waved good night to Hiram as his car pulled out of the tiny gravel lot behind the crumbling three-story. Grasping her car key's "Panic" button like it was Excalibur, she raced shadows the distance to her car, last in the lot. Once in the driver's seat, she was quick to lock its doors. Lord only knew to what crimes against single females this desolate street had borne dispassionate witness on nights such as this. For a woman alone in the dark, as she was, there was no such thing as being too cautious.

She started the engine and threw her Ford Escort into gear, happy to be a couple hundred dollars richer tonight. The vehicle gargled and lurched huffing out onto the macadam, an apologetic beast with nearly treadless tires, with strips of duct tape holding its rear window together.

Hiram was a sweet man, and Mera's two nights a week of nakedness with him in more than the literal sense, the most instructive experiences of her life. Everything from the instructions he gave while she was earning, to the gentle way he guided her body into positions that coaxed forth her most radiant work, spoke of a genteel masculinity that she'd thought long lost to extinction. Despite the volume of onlookers that typically attended their spectacle, self-consciousness that would have debilitated a lesser woman remained a stranger to Mera. In that place, on those nights, her inhibitions fell away as surely as the clothes she shed, her chrysalis of limitations dissipating. With all attention upon her, plotting her every curve, charting her every physical convexity, describing every circle comprising her, Mera took center stage and gave the room all the kinetic visuals she could muster, all that the starscape of studious eyes encircling her could ever hope to behold. But Hiram's two were the only stars in that galaxy that could make her feel nude when they shone upon her. In an odd way that she could neither share nor explain to anyone, the time that she spent with him felt almost like making love.

There'd been fifty extra dollars in tonight's envelope that Hiram hadn't said a word about putting there. He knew from the chats he and Mera enjoyed while she dressed at the end of each evening, after his students were gone, that times were harder for some than for others. A sweet man; one who had thus far passed up every single opportunity to try something foolish with the shapely reawakened jogger ten years his junior. Her wedding ring glared up at her from the steering wheel, admonishing as she contemplated her presumptive reaction to him, should Hiram ever stop ignoring the possibility. Whether such an act on his part would likelier ruin the relationship between him and her, or between her and her husband, Mera refused to ponder.

As she refused to do at the conclusion of her every visit.

Mera thought of Hank and wished as she had a dozen times throughout the evening's course that time would amend his opinions of the work she did down at that place out near the airport. As part-time work went, there were plenty of gigs worse than her being an artists' model, and more than a few of those would also have involved her taking off her clothes.

But she knew that her nudity formed but one root of her husband's unrest. The fact that she appeared to be enjoying the work was the true crux of the matter, that when she returned home after each modeling class, she came without a trace of that self-loathing shame that the self-righteous touted as "decency." For the past eight months now, she'd bubbled home two nights a week, effervescent, and in more than the fiduciary sense, enriched by evenings well-spent. It was that other sense, that warm little extra that Hank had never been willing to give, that threatened him.

To Hank's thinking, being paid to get naked translated to his wife's enjoyment of being ogled and desired by men other than him. Mera could only imagine what tragic operas his mind's eye had composed to the notion of her lapping up other men's affectionate attention like sundae syrup. That he hadn't come down to Hiram's studio, reeking of rye alcohol, and threatened to do the man harm continued to surprise Mera, and she grinned only momentarily at the thought before chiding herself for the unfairness to Hank.

They'd had their share of marital problems, and would surely have more before his hair and hers went to gray, but to call Hank a monster was to unjustly malign him. Having her sister staying with them following Angela's loss of her latest job and living situation had not only strained relationships between Mera and Hank, but between her and her sister, as well. Angela's unfortunate pairing of recovering alcoholic and flirtatious nature borne of early and generous pubescence had cost her big sister more than a few hours of sleep. Mera knew that Angela had coasted as far through life on physical attractiveness as was probably possible. As her only surviving family, it fell to Mera to awaken the girl to this fact before it was too late, before she fell into the wrong man's bed and forfeited more of herself than she could afford to lose.

Mera pulled the Ford onto the gravel outside the camper, still mildly amused by the mental image of Hank's staggering into Hiram's studio some night in search of an ass to kick. She chided herself a final time for thinking such things, knowing she had much for which to be grateful to her husband. Hank hadn't hesitated to agree to take her sister in when she'd turned up on their doorstep malnourished and owning nothing but the clothes on her back. Throughout Angela's stay of several months that were supposed to have been a mere couple of weeks, he had never complained. When she came through the door tonight, he would probably pout, he would probably interrogate Mera about her evening. In the face of her refusal to feel badly about her earnings this night, he would probably storm out to the local watering hole and toss back a few with his idiot friends. But if Mera knew one thing about her Hank, it was that for all his bluster, there wasn't a violent or unfaithful bone in the man's body.

THE GIFT OF INFINITE MIDNIGHT

Lucien's clothes looked better on the dead, hairless boy with the kohl-stained eyelids than they did on him. The cooling corpse grinned up at Lucien from the sticky motel bedsheets, seeming as grateful for those gifts of black satin and suede as he had for the gift of Lucien's mouth upon him. Idiot. Moonlight dripped between the heavy drapes covering the room's only window. Here and there, crimson splotches like red wine staining the sheets glistened in its frigid glow.

They were not red wine stains.

He might have killed the effeminate youth even if Lucien hadn't come away from this encounter two thousand dollars richer. He might have done it for the sheer enchanting glee of it, just as he'd done with his younger sister Carina's kitten as a child. The animal, like the pale, cane-thin boy, had committed the sin of once too often testing Lucien's patience. It mattered not whether his irritation came in the form of a fluffy, wide-eyed little sack of piss with a growing fondness for urinating into Lucien's shoes, or in that of a hairless queer hellbent on carrying his vampire fetish too far. Lucien's ire, once roused, was a bloodhound. Relentless, its satisfaction it would demand by gnawing day and night at his mental fringes until Lucien sat convinced that his very sanity depended upon doing whatever should silence it.

The dead boy's grin, one that Lucien found utterly unpalatable for its grace and beauty, lay frozen upon the delicate face. It looked exactly as Lucien had imagined it the day he received the boy's first blood-smeared correspondence to him.

*****

Skillful storytellers as a collective would always be Lucien's favorite kind of people. Among their more enviable qualities, there was that wonderful ability to suspend disbelief in others, to yarn convincingly on people and places and happenings both real and surreal. Even more laudable was to accomplish such undertakings with the confidence that audiences will sit up and heed the tale and hunger for more, no matter how wildly improbable, downright impossible the topic might seem. Confidence was the crux of it; the courage to damn popular social convention and speak, write, think openly, even at risk of being thought "irreverent" or "unorthodox."

Ever since his adolescence, sitting with Carina at their uncle's feet, listening to tales of ghost riders and restless spirits said to inhabit their town on foggy nights, Lucien had admired this quality. The passage of years would see others grow to appreciate that quality in Lucien as well. Throughout his novelist's career, his horror fiction had certainly topped enough bestsellers lists and earned him enough literary awards and honorariums to convince the world that Lucien de Rochard was a master of his craft.

At age twenty-nine, magazine articles dubbed him "Horror Writing's Next King." The appellation smacked as much of humor as of pretentiousness for the unsubtle duality of it. By the time Lucien turned thirty-two, he'd authored two short horror collections, as well as the Splintered Soul Trilogy, which told the visceral, generations-long tale of the DuChamp vampire clan. Unlike many of his writing contemporaries, Lucien favored vampirism as a story subject. In taverns after midnight, he frequently heard the confessions of fellow authors, whispered admissions that they would shudder to attempt building on a centuries-old myth. Or one that's been, in Carina's words, "so exhaustively commercialized." Lucien rarely balked at a challenge, though, and there existed few greater challenges to a writer than breathing welcome vigor into jaded subjects. "Horror Writing's Next King" was nothing if not brazenly confident in his own ability to spin dusty cobwebs into lace gauntlets.

An inevitable downside to royal status, of course, is that no king's court is without its fool. The murdered sycophant in the motel bed seemed proof enough of that. If what the dead boy had desired of him was a soulmate who suffered fools gladly, then Lucien de Rochard was a poor selection indeed.

By the time tonight's full moon was risen, Lucien lamented knowing that the kid called himself Saint Sebastian and had seen "Nosferatu" sixty times. The less humanity he acknowledged in the pale youth, the simpler it would have been for Lucien to perform the deed for which he'd been paid. However, Saint Sebastian had provided Lucien more than sufficient cause to oblige him. The youth's initiative and his mania both found voice less through his written musings, as through his presentation of them: Saint Sebastian penned his every correspondence to Lucien in human blood. He claimed the blood was his own, a thought that Lucien found exhilarating despite himself.

O, Incandescent Mister de Rochard:

I'm an affectionate fan who wishes to know if you are a vampire. Your writing drips with such realism as only a person drawing from personal experience could bring to the page. If, sir, I'm correct in this assumption, then gladly will I pay you to bite me, as I DESPERATELY wish to be a vampire. I am willing to travel to meet you one night soon, in a quiet, moonlit crypt of your choosing if you will grant me your assistance in achieving what it is I seek.

Respondez si vous plait,
Saint Sebastian

*****

If it was self-assuredness that Lucien admired most in others, then whimsy was the trait that he abhorred above all else. Particularly Saint Sebastian's brand of whimsy. It pestered Lucien like an itch demanding to be scratched, but incapable of ever being pacified.

Such displays of ignorance always made him laugh, but never made him smile. It made him want to split a fool's head, snap a fool's neck, tie a fool to a tree and kick him to death. Old stereotypes grew no less infuriating with time. The author of a novel about a serial killer never got asked whether his basement was crowded with the corpses of unfortunates murdered at his hand for the sake of literary research. People usually knew better than that, and those who didn't know sometimes founded churches, but at least *they* were easily identifiable. Saint Sebastian's kind of fool, the deceptive, dishonest sort that masquerades as a loyal fan while perpetuating the notion that you are what you write, would always be the bane of Lucien's existence.

And so, at age thirty-seven, all but bankrupted by two ex-wives and an affinity for opiates, Lucien de Rochard stood rinsing blood from under his fingernails in a cracked motel washbasin. He'd actually done it; he'd actually *bitten* the little poser. Not merely bitten him, but gagged him, tethered the younger man's bony wrists behind him in that motel bed and torn into that supple tract of porcelain flesh like a runaway chainsaw. He hadn't planned for things to go down that way. But something dark and betraying had grabbed hold of Lucien in that moment; something black and deceptive that hungered for the sweet warmth of Saint Sebastian's blood spraying Lucien's face. Something suspecting no one would even miss the Goth boy. So rather than visiting the intended light piercing of the skin upon him, Lucien instead bit rabidly, punched his teeth through tissue and pulp as Saint Sebastian screamed into his gag and fishtailed around beneath him, sweaty and feral with his agony.

Is it wrong, Lucien wondered, to relish the act of using one's teeth to rip open the throat of another human being? Perhaps, he admitted to himself—but loathing Saint Sebastian came so easily to Lucien that he'd forgiven himself before the dying boy finally stopped twitching.

Shards of the light bulb that had exploded all over the bathroom when he flipped the wall switch swirled into the drain. Lucien felt ready for a drink. He needed something to get the taste of red meat out of his mouth.

Lucien spat a scrap of Saint Sebastian's skin into the washbasin. He didn't desire any such mementos of this evening's events. Reminder enough of what he'd done lie in the ruined bed, in the desperate longing contained in the boy's gaze when at last, they'd met at the truck stop twelve miles back. Oh, how he had loved Lucien! Instantly, passionately, wholeheartedly loved him the way people love angels and infants. Blindly, dangerously, he'd loved. Saint Sebastian's love was the kind that thought nothing of checking into motels with strangers who registered under pseudonyms and left false license plate data with desk clerks.

Well, tough shit, as far as Lucien was concerned. He hadn't asked Saint Sebastian to fawn all over him like a prancing schoolgirl. Lucien's passion was for writing, not for jerking the cocks of pale baby Goths.

Lucien wondered just how long afterimages of the dead boy's face would remain in his head. He would forever loathe the boy for the way his ignominious death molested Lucien's senses.

*****

Beyond the motel windows, a full Savannah moon beckoned to Lucien, splashing illumination over Saint Sebastian. Moonlight gathered in pools at the trunks of trees resembling splintered bone fragments, rotted leviathan fangs in the blue-black night. Lucien tossed open the room's garish canvas curtains, inviting lunar illumination into the murder scene to bear witness to his crime. He massaged the hand he'd used to muffle the blood-soaked cries as he'd opened the dying boy's jugular with his teeth. His throat burned. Endorphins had set his extremities trembling as if he'd just concluded a marathon. Perhaps he'd go see about that drink now. It wouldn't buy him lifetime security, but two grand was two grand. Two thousand dollars cash would buy a hell of a lot of black label.

Saint Sebastian, however, demanded a final bit of his attention first, and damn if Lucien wasn't going to bid him a proper farewell. Uncorking a tiny bottle of shitty brandy he'd received as a Christmas gift, Lucien sloshed the bedsheets with amber liquid. He hated brandy.

Lucien tossed into the rumpled bed the remaining third of the cigarette he was smoking. Retrieving a hammer from the duffel bag he'd brought along, Lucien used it to bash in the room's only smoke detector. Its plastic casing splintered as the blow smashed the detector to the floor with a sound that might have startled guests in the adjacent rooms, had there been any other guests.

He couldn't let motel management discover the corpse lying there with the glinting wound chewed in its throat, the teeth marks perforating its Adam's apple. The only findings left behind for authorities to inaccurately conjecture over would be the charred remains of an adult male that no one had even seen enter the motel. Sure, some industrious officer seeking a promotion might sift through the ashes for clues. Somehow, this ambitious young detective might even learn that the corpse had burned wearing garments of satin and leather. It would be assumed that Lucien, having signed in wearing precisely such an ensemble had burned to death smoking in bed. One more drunk-ass drifter turned up dead in a motel. Hell, it probably wouldn't get reported at all.

Something grisly inside him born of contempt for Saint Sebastian felt tempted to stay for a moment, watch the body begin to smolder as the flames licked him intimately. Only barely did Lucien resist that urge. Time to make his escape before the smell of smoke could attract any attention.

"Leaving me so soon, lover?" he heard as his hand twisted the doorknob. Lucien gaped like a dimwit at the wet, eager grin greeting him from the unburned bed. The faintly luminous eyes so full of love. So hungry.

Ravenous.

Saint Sebastian sat up in the gloom, the wound on his throat all but vanished. A smattering of blood along his jaw formed the only evidence that violence of any kind had transpired. As a younger man, Lucien might have flung open the hotel door and run screaming into the night. But he was not the young man he'd once been, and couldn't run like he once could.

"No. No, I murdered you," a lightheaded Lucien whined, "I lined my pockets with your money and I murdered you. Gladly."

"Oh, dear Mister de Rochard," the pale hairless boy smiled, dragging on the cigarette Lucien had tossed into bed, "Lucien. You can't rape the willing." He blew a smoke ring toward Lucien.

Cemented to the floor. Trapped beneath the weight of those eyes. Lucien croaked, "What in hell are you?" Knowing the answer. Fearing the boy's reply. Christ, he'd bitten this kid, this *thing*. Tasted its blood. Swallowed it.

Ingested. Lucien had ingested vampire blood.

"I'm your saint." The boy told him, responding in a tone that mocked Lucien; the tone of a parent placating a fussy toddler. He went on, "I know you sought to violate me, nothing more. But I forgive you. Believe me, you are far from being the first to try what you tried. It stands to reason that you certainly won't be the last."

Forgive? Lucien wondered who the hell this punk thought he was talking to.

"Well so what if I tried to bilk you? You begged me for it, writing me, upping the dollar amount with every letter you sent. You think anyone else would have cut you a squarer deal than mine, you're fooling yourself, kid. You got off easy." Lucien found himself speaking with the conviction of a terminal man, despite the terror seeking to arrest his air as well as his words. He hated himself for lacking the good sense to faint.

"I came to you seeking knowledge," Saint Sebastian said.

"Well, I hate to break it to you, young man, but there ain't no Easter bunny. Writing about vampires has earned me some fat paychecks and some good blowjobs, but there's no such motherfucking thing as motherfucking vampires between here and Hell, and you know it as well as I do!"

Saint Sebastian sidled closer to Lucien and snatched the older man in a hug. He could have been hugging an infirm old woman for the gentleness of the gesture. Lucien found he could not avoid the embrace. His limbs refused to obey his command to crack the kid across his girly jaw. Then Saint Sebastian smiled at Lucien; a close-range smile allowing Lucien to take indisputable note of the boy's canines, how arced and terribly sharp they looked, how the moonlight glinted along their perfect tips. Lucien could not recall whether they'd looked like that all along.

“Of course there’s no such thing as vampires, or so society would dictate,” Saint Sebastian sniffed, again utilizing that tone of one addressing a dullard. “Or so *we* would have the Homo sapiens believe. But how much of what you know do you *really know*, Lucien?”

Then Saint Sebastian performed the first of several acts that would hurt Lucien that night.

Lucien’s world drained away on agonizing currents of bliss-pain that he would come to crave. Of this, Saint Sebastian assured him. The arcing of Lucien’s canines, the rising lust light behind his eyes, the pearlized luminescence of his skin: he would embrace these once the change in him began. Saint Sebastian would wait patiently for as long as necessary. After all, they had moonlight and eternity to share together.

SLOW BURN

An "oral fixation." That's what her therapist called it. Darcy preferred "most welcome addiction."

The stigma surrounding it hadn't mattered to her in years. Her mother's opinion that "Ladies of quality don't" might have meant more if Darcy knew that the woman had enjoyed even a moment's ecstasy in her fifty-six years. Doubtful, though, of a woman who rarely put down her Bible even to hug her only daughter.

Her black-Lycra-clad bartender watched, enthralled, as Darcy worked. Darcy closed her eyes and flicked her tongue across the moistened tip of the object of her affection. Its musky aroma anointed her nostrils. Sucking gingerly, she drew its flavors between her teeth, across her tongue. Her mouth formed a tight seal born of years spent perfecting this technique. As with the difference between fucking and making love, attention to technique was vital if satisfaction was to be hers. Couldn't spend this one too quickly.

To hell with those who wrinkled their noses over her "filthy" habit. Health risks be damned, the warm presence between her lips felt too damn good to be given up. Besides, as vices went, there were far worse things available these days to a twenty-seven-year-old single female living in New York City. But unmatched was Darcy's skill at her chosen distraction, and having to occasionally wash its evidence from her hair and clothing posed the smallest of sacrifices. On the contrary, some delicious dirtiness about that aspect of it not only thrilled, but also amused her.

Lovelight burned in the luminous orange fireworks that showered every time Darcy tapped her smoke. Smoldering like fever, the cigarette's glowing ember kissed Darcy's face with ambient heat that swelled as it neared her lips. No small titillation lie in knowing that such pervasive, primal ardor could live in a thing so confined, so visually unremarkable. She fancied it, as she fancied herself, the ultimate masquerade.

Darcy sucked smoke from the unfiltered shaft between her lips. A full-body "Mmmm," the kind once reserved for the sweep of a knowledgeable tongue between vulva and anus, thrummed through her.

Ambrosia.

Tonight her palate was a clitoris, teased to ultra-sensitivity by the cherry oak bite of velvet smoke like ejaculate flavoring her tongue. Tonight her mouth was a second cunt, lubed with aroused anticipation of its every penetration by the deftly-circumcised cocks of lovers mentholated, lovers spiced with Damiana and clove. Beneath her dress, her sex was a pouting tulip in dew-slick bloom.

Her bartender raked a hand through his curls before approaching Darcy with the Cuba Libre she ordered. She'd felt him watching her lips adore her savory, paper-skinned paramour, refusing to interrupt her even to present her requested cocktail. He wanted so badly to fuck her that the poor man was sweating. His tented pants were the dead giveaway, and Darcy's urge to taunt him with a quick and beckoning smile got the best of her. Backing away, he managed to stumble over his own feet before returning his own nervous grin. She waited until he'd moved beyond earshot before she laughed.

*****

If he got her naked tonight, Wynntree would bite her. He'd bite her on her right pelvis where the artful flaring of her luscious hip joined her thigh. It might sting at first, but would grow to feel natural to her over time. If he got her naked.

Her ass, in all its forbidden magnificence would grow accustomed to his probing. His balls would drip with her heat as he took her bent over bathtubs and sofachairs. They'd call it a stretching exercise, him sinking his swollen member between her asscheeks, her gasping at its thickness as he lurched forward again and again, stuffing her tightest orifice. He would bind her in leather restraints, dress her in miniskirts, blindfold her in the leash and collar that he would purchase just for her. If he got her naked tonight.

She would offer her breasts to him, young and firm, her sacrificial tribute to him, her bronze-muscled messiah. She would worship kneeling at the altar of his massive cock, its honey-smeared curvature glinting suggestively, inches from her voluptuous lips, her expert tongue. At his whim, she would accompany him on business excursions posing as his adopted daughter. She would suck his business partners dry of semen while he watched from across the room, fucking his favorite call girl with inebriated gusto. Sometimes, if she swallowed after draining each erection, he would allow her to self-induce an orgasm for his partners to crowd around and watch.

Veils of exotic smoke filling the stately clubhouse did nothing to mask his simmering cruelty: He wanted to fuck her violently. He wanted to wrestle her onto the brass-and-mahogany bar, rip her dress, and attack her the way a cougar tears into a gazelle. Unlike words, body language never whispered. The way his gaze kept sliding from her face to snatch at her breasts like hands that she could almost feel; his tremulous smile and fingers; the unsubtle shifting of his weight from one foot to the other: all of these added up to his wanting to maul her like a carnivore.

Darcy decided the magenta velvet minidress and stiletto pumps had been an excellent choice after all.

Wynntree packed his Dakota Thames pipe with Honey Cavendish tobacco without taking his eyes off the dark-haired beauty before him. He favored Dakotas over Royce grade pipes. Most pipe aficionados he knew fancied Royces, he told her, for their infinitesimal surface imperfections and six-week sweet-curing duration. Younger club members tended toward them as well, their selection process typically fettered by ignorance. Wynntree's Smoker's Club membership, however, spanned decades, dating back to an age when he'd have looked less fatherly beside the young lady currently enjoying his company. He could boast familiarity with every grade of tobacco pipe in existence. These days, Wynntree's only desire was for a good

Honey Cavendish smoke in his aged-briar Dakota at the end of the day; and for the occasional lay.

"So tell me, dear," Wynntree said, "Have you ever been to one of these Smokers' Socials before?" His tone wove the sound of creaking bedsprings into the words. How a woman with such enigmatic eyes and lips so sweetly suited to giving head could be single, he would never fathom.

"It's my first time tonight," she lied in those same seductive Brazilian tones that for over twenty minutes now, had maintained the erection in Wynntree's cotton twills. God, she even *smelled* fuckable, standing on her toes to shout in competition with the roaring laughter and conversations of other smokers. Heaven was standing there watching her release smoke through pursed lips that surely were a direct and perfect representation of her pussy. Hell too, was this.

Wynntree moved a step closer. Leering at her, he probably sought to effect suaveness, but only looked smug. He *would* get her naked tonight. Damn if this one was getting away from him!

"First time tonight?" Wynntree parroted. "Well then, I guess I'll have to be very gentle, won't I?" His brassy chuckle then, self-congratulating, befitting a man convinced he is a great wit.

It was the lady's turn now to leer. "No, you won't." Suggestions unspoken and libidinous in her eyes stroked his mind and cock with the promise of a hot, snug throat, of tight pussy and brown, bucking hips.

"Shall we, then?" Wynntree grinned, offering the lady his arm. His eyes spoke sagas about his expectations for tonight. Implications of steel hoops, leather-clenched wrists, icy clamps swam in them. Whenever he blinked, one could almost hear the whipcracks of his paddles and flogs and sweaty palms stinging captive flesh, summoning bruises to brand sensitive feminine tissues. These were not eyes accustomed to watching a woman's lips form the word "no," Darcy knew. But how did a green-eyed brunette with waist-length hair and 38-24-34 endowments tell the man who's spent the past hour-and-a-half buying her cocktails that she's tired of sex?

“I need to make a little detour between here and our exit,” Darcy replied, nodding toward the ladies’ room. She needed his face removed from her sight for a few moments. Thinking was too damn hard with those mercenary eyes molesting her. She flipped her cigarette package closed and placed it beside her ashtray before hurrying to the ladies’ room.

The special hell of it was that Darcy *wanted* Wynntree. Older men held salacious sorcery in their stride and confident manner, as far as Darcy was concerned, and they always had. She *wanted* to desire his nimble hands beneath her dress. She *wanted* to surrender to the overpowering urge to smear her lips with the musk between his thighs. She *wanted* to feel him looming behind her, huffing raggedly, driving forward until her bed pillows could no longer contain her moans.

The trouble was, she didn’t *want* to want to.

Physical intimacy seemed such a chore these days; an unwarranted tedium best left to preteens seeking merciful emancipation from virginity’s social disease. A woman had to be a fucking twelfth-generation contortionist to please today’s man. To hell with a little petting in the backseat of his car nowadays; offer a guy anything short of a steel-caged bondage-based trapeze fuck on the first date, and all too many of them acted as if they’d been shortchanged. Nope. Too much exertion, too much sweat, too much goddamned etiquette involved in it for Darcy. She favored the internal caresses of tobacco and flame.

Life was too fucking short to be suffered unfulfilled. She felt it every waking minute, burning away like a fuse. Going up in smoke. This made quality everything over quantity. For all man’s possessions and status, when death embraced each of us, life experiences were the only things we could take with us into whatever night awaited beyond this world. Meaningless, uninspired carnality, the kind that somehow always felt rote despite the frequent perversions fostered by meaningless, uninspired fuckmates, simply wasn’t in Darcy’s plan anymore. Not when nicotine love stung the spirit so sweetly. She’d experienced enough wantonness to desire more than that.

In her fierce youth, Darcy took lovers the way she now takes smokes, spending them emotionally until they crumbled to detritus, collecting their uncharismatic echoes in fugues like ashtrays. In her adulthood, she still appreciated the inferno beneath a lover's smoldering exterior. Darcy simply took the analogy and her appreciation for it more literally than most women.

Darcy flushed the toilet and washed her hands. On her way back to the bar, she practiced her excuse for declining to join Wynntree for the evening. By the time she rejoined him, she had it down cold. As she approached, Wynntree swiveled on his bar stool and grinned. Darcy shrieked and nearly lost consciousness. The cigarette package she'd left on the bar lay crushed and empty, cast aside like a used Kleenex.

Fighting to speak calmly, she asked "Jacob . . . what have you done?"

Pinched into the corner of his mouth, Darcy's last unfiltered cigarette bobbed haphazardly as he spoke. It burned unevenly, betraying that it had been lit improperly, due either to Wynntree's carelessness or his ignorance. He dragged too hard on it, his silver-stubbled jowls collapsing on each inhalation like a man seeking to suck a golf ball through a drinking straw. The cigarette looked mortified dangling from his thin lips. Darcy swore she could hear it pleading to be released from its indignity.

"Stole one of your smokes. Wanted to see if these things tasted as awful as I remember. Haven't smoked anything but my Dakota in years. You don't mind, do you, love?"

Necrotic ashes sloughed away from its ember like poor paramours falling out of Darcy's life, accumulating amidst the indistinguishable dunes in her ashtray.

The tears that sprang to her reddening eyes seared their sockets. Red murder howled against the inside of Darcy's skull, seeming to gouge the bone, at the sight of the cigarette, once her beacon proudly personifying refined rage, brought so low. She felt the way a champion pugilist's wife would feel watching as he was pummeled bloody. Wynntree's smirk was odious, an abomination, like forcing a father to watch his teenage daughter give head.

Her unfiltered lover's disgrace was a spoor that Darcy could faintly taste on each breath she drew. That Wynntree had perpetrated this callousness so reflexively only compounded its savagery. Knowing it had been no calculated maneuver, no deliberately executed offense, but a goddamned whim, and that after this, he *still* intended to fuck her tonight. . . these made it worse than rape.

"So are we off then, angel?" Wynntree asked, puffing fetid smoke.

Taking his hand in hers, she nibbled the meaty thumb, stealing a taste of him. Ogling his crotch as she was, Darcy didn't have to say a word, but did, leaving him no room to misinterpret her designs. Something evil touched her grin, serving only to excite Wynntree further, and betray to him that this lady had plans of her own for them tonight.

"Yes, hon," she murmured against his cheek, "We're off and running."

Wynntree settled their tab, tipping the bartender fifty big ones the way he always did on nights when his getting some pussy before the evening was over seemed a foregone conclusion. Darcy accepted his invitation to accompany him home for the evening. He had a hungry one on his hands, and the sooner he got them both out of their clothes, the sooner he could push her to her knees and acquaint her with the new lifestyle he had planned for her.

*****

The candles Wynntree had promised to light lay heaped and forgotten in a corner of his bedroom. Moonlight frosted his paunch, his doughy nakedness. Nude and breathtaking, Darcy sat beside him, luscious legs crossed. She'd persuaded Wynntree to have his driver stop along the way, and drew a filtered clove cigarette from one of the half-dozen newly-purchased packs that now tenanted her purse. She'd be needing them tonight. All of them.

The leather cuffs he'd intended to tighten around Darcy's wrists and ankles secured Wynntree to the four corners of his queen-sized bed. He bit into the red rubber ball he'd intended to gag her with, still grinning like a fool, still anticipating a night of the kind of perverse pleasures implicated by Darcy's minidress and perfect valentine of an ass.

"I know what you want," she told him disinterestedly, lighting her smoke, "and I'll give it to you if you still want it after my lesson is complete. Once I'm satisfied that you've absorbed the lesson, I'll devour you in tiny little love bites." Her eyes smiled at him. Her mouth did not.

She stroked his blushing genitals, feeling them tighten beneath her fingertips. Confident that his undivided attention was hers, Darcy bent to blow clove-flavored smoke up his nostrils. Wynntree squirmed as she combed the stripe of silvery hair decorating his stomach with her nails, lingering at his navel. She gave his cock a squeeze, testing its firmness. He was ready.

"All right, let's begin. Lesson number one," Darcy's eyes quit smiling. Wynntree's did too as she removed the cigarette from her mouth and seized his cock. If ever a circumstance had arisen that not only justified, but *necessitated* a brief relapse into the wantonness of her youth, then certainly here was such a circumstance. His insensitivity would be atoned for, and Darcy's debased smoke, avenged.

"Next time you want one of my smokes," she began, "You. Fucking. *Ask.* First!" Darcy brought the livid orange eye of God closer to Wynntree's face. His blood-rimmed eyes reflected its hue, gleaming like strange jewels. His manhood stiffened in her hands. Seconds into their threesome, he began to scream for her.

Love bites. Searing red-hot love bites. The ember hissed as if with grudging affection, as Darcy ground it out in the eye of Wynntree's cock.

LORD OF ALL THAT GLITTERS

Tahseen finds the loft-style studio's only windowsill sooty yet cool beneath her backside. That anyone was leasing any part of this warehouse-district four-story was news to her. Local legendry that still surrounds the place and its past as a crematorium had hurt its market desirability as well as that of neighboring addresses, and had kept it largely untenanted for years. Tahseen stretches, arching her bare back, supposing that perhaps some truth lie in the adage about time healing all wounds. God knows she needs it to be true, after her unexpected performance here tonight.

The night steals a taste of moist skin, its breezes lapping reverently at her tender nipples and still-tingling sex. Across the room, the door to the refrigerator where Myles chills beer for visitors hangs opened, and Myles, a sinewy masterpiece of angled sepia, stands relishing the coolness therein. "A five-minute break" he'd promised her hours ago; then they'd continue the photo shoot. Five orgasms later, the camera lies as forgotten as the clothes she wore over here. Phantoms of her photographer's hands frolic over her arcs. Myles licks Tahseen's payment from his lips.

"Delight Your Man With Nude, Sensual You," read the classified ad that lured her here. Tahseen lounges ravaged and sticky, imagining her lover's eyes as he peruses the personalized erotic pictorial that will be her gift to him; every page featuring her Burmese mystique, each picture's thousand words speaking of unabashed lust. On those weekends when his band tours out of town, these photos taken tonight will remind her Andrew that one-night stands make poor substitute for what exotica awaits his return. They'll testify to Tahseen's devotion to a fiancé she didn't think of once while Myles was inside her.

"Whore," the night whispers to Tahseen, demanding explanation for the taste spicing her tongue; the flavor of the naked man standing halfway inside the refrigerator. Clutching her cardamom-colored shoulders, Tahseen laments her indiscretions tonight. She thinks of Andrew and wants to die. She watches Myles stalk toward her and wants to live.

Accustomed by the benefits of trim ankles, taut buttocks, and shimmering black hair to propositions from the lusting populace both male and female alike, she wonders what has compelled her to forego typical casual flirtation for infidelity with *this* man after rejecting countless others. She wonders what makes her already want him inside her again.

More than twenty minutes have passed without a word between them. Myles sweeps cottony cocoa-colored dreadlocks away from his ruggedly-hewn face, overstepping emptied Trojan packages and spent condoms, to hand Tahseen an opened bottle of lager. He holds the bottle just below his waist, near the glossy espresso column of his cock. Tahseen's hand brushes the taut muscle, lingering as she receives his offering. Draining their bottles in silence, they stare down the accusing night sky as if watching for the arrival of angels come to Hell's Kitchen to punish their abandon.

Tahseen finds herself sweating despite the cooling night. Restless hunger licks her between the thighs, leaving her feverish; starving to fuck again. Squeezed between Myles, her hard-muscled Adonis, and thoughts of Andrew, she contemplates the loaded glare of the moon as Myles's fingers thread her hair. If there be angels seeking to punish her indiscretions this night, then let them come. Let them arrive to find her every orifice anointed with Myles's seed.

Enough rest, demands her full-body shiver. Tahseen's knees kiss the floorboards. Her molestations claim his firmness. Myles groans and stiffens as she swallows him.

Her mouth is a womb. Her mouth is an awesome cherry-peel machine reverently wringing forth the sacrament from her lord of licentiousness. His fingers winding her hair into handles, the growing urgency in his thrusts, his furtive oaths wafting away like blue bubbles into the night set Tahseen's skin burning.

Bathed in pheromone-laced fucksweat, her brow glistens, feeling scorched with her efforts.

Tahseen's vision swims as his pearlescent tide swells. Washed beyond coherence by his frothing eruption, Tahseen can only grunt her assent as Myles sinks to his knees behind her, presses his chest against her back, and impales her anew.

*****

Myles is speaking to her, firing incomprehensible words the understanding of which, her senses insist on deflecting. A strange kind of vertigo has reduced him to a caramel-colored blob. He feels heavy; a slick and burning weight forcing air from her lungs, further bathing her in the pheromone of his sweat and saliva. She smiles through the searing pain assailing her skin as his softening penis withdraws from her anus. Strangely, her unsated feeling lingers. Her thoughts and memories of Andrew do not.

"Thanks, sugar," she would hear, were she capable of understanding, "You're the first meal I've had in weeks. And you were delicious every inch, without a doubt. You saved my life." Could she see straight, Tahseen would notice something different and discomfiting about his teeth. Inebriated by the bioelectrical emissions he's spent all evening drinking from her orgasms, Myles stands, lifting her along. It is time he finishes immortalizing her as his advertisement promised.

The affronted scream of aged gears summoned to action splits the evening's calm as Myles leads her to the elevator cage that carried her to his fourth-floor studio. Tahseen is contented enough to follow wherever he may take her. She doesn't even realize that neither she nor Myles have dressed. It feels too good to be nude right now. His arms around her as the elevator descends to a destination he has not yet shared with her, his lips creeping along her neck feel too good, too right for her to concern herself with asking questions to which answers will surely come in good time.

"So, the time has come for a little confession on my part. I confess that I tend to fall in love with all my subjects," the scaly creature shedding Myles's skin says, leading Tahseen nude into the larger of two rooms leading from that black-painted brick one which has served as their fucknest all evening. He says it smiling that bashful indicted smile from whence all Tahseen's infidelities sprang; the one that makes him look so unspeakably fuckable. If only she could see it now. She might find herself galvanized by a different set of inclinations, could she view the thickening hide, the explosion of crescent-shaped needles currently replacing the pearly whites of which she'd been so enamored upon first meeting him.

"I love my work. Positioning each subject for my cameras; lining up the shots, choosing the props, the backdrops. And please, believe me when I tell you that I sincerely love each lady. Each lady is my passion when she's here, just as you are my passion tonight," he goes on, "When I have them here on their knees, on their backs, in my mouth, I make them glow and for those few moments, they're mine. *You* are mine. The hard part is having to smile graciously and give you all back to your boyfriends and husbands once a shoot is done."

The room they enter is low-ceilinged and cozy. Its hardwood flooring is lacquered to a bloodlike hue. Three rows of ivory shelves deck all but one of its four walls, and luxurious blue velvet drapes each of these. Spaced along these velvet-festooned shelves, diamonds of varying shapes and sizes wink at Myles and Tahseen in the meager lighting, not that her eyes are obeying her demands that they focus enough to discern her surroundings. An inscribed gold plate is set before each gem, not that they are visible to Tahseen's severely dilated pupils. An expansive and aged-looking iron door is the only adornment reserved for the room's fourth wall, which is composed entirely of firebricks.

The steel sliding tray behind the iron door opening under Myles' telekinetic direction is human-sized, reinforced to support up to four-hundred-eighty pounds. Myles hefts Tahseen in his arms and places her upon it. Even as the notion of some wrongness unfolding here breaks upon her, Tahseen's limbs feel too heavy to lift. Even if she could grasp the danger of her situation as more than a fleeting flash skirting the periphery of her mind, she could offer no resistance. The sedative contained in the sweat and saliva of the creature she knows only as "Myles" has anesthetized her too efficiently for her to object to being entombed in bricks.

"You'll glow too, precious," Myles tells Tahseen, smiling reassuringly with his newer, sharper teeth as he slides her into the grave-like enclosure built into his wall, and bolts the iron door closed.

Nourished by Tahseen's energies, Myles is strong once again. Strong enough to ably wield the gifts granted to his species centuries ago. Myles concentrates, murmurs in that dead language which has served him for over a century. Tahseen's scream is a scarring thing that rouses tears to his eyes as spontaneous flames that burn hotter than the most efficient crematorium engulf her.

*****

It occurs to Myles hours later as his mental energies clean out the tomblike space, that even her ashes are beautiful. He chants the dead language as he works extracts carbon from those ashes. No matter how often he commands it, the sight of human detritus shifting and parting and rearranging itself unassisted by his hands always offers him an impressive spectacle. The ageless creature spends more than an hour working to compress the roiling globule of carbon that forms between his splayed fingertips; crushing, shaping it beyond human capability, visiting hundreds of pounds of telekinetic pressure per square centimeter upon it. Though exhausted, though washed in sweat, the creature soon draws Myles's cheeks wide with its sated grin.

He will not keep the photos he took of Tahseen tonight for keepsakes. They will burn as do those of all his subjects, as do the subjects themselves. What remembrance could ever compare with the diamond that embodies each woman's feminine essence, the jewel created by the sheer force of his will and sorcery? The gemstone created this night from what precious carbon existed in his latest love is no mere memento of Tahseen. The gemstone upon which the creature known to so many women only as "Myles" places a longing kiss *is* Tahseen. . .what greater tribute than this could ever honor the woman?

Myles places Tahseen upon the highest shelf at his back. She will rest there, between diamonds bearing the respective nameplates of "Lisa" and "Angelique." Tomorrow, he will fashion a nameplate bearing the name of his collection's most recent acquisition. Tonight however, exhaustion has left him capable of little except sleep.

"Giving my ladies back to lovers who underappreciate them has always been the most difficult, most loathsome part of what I do," Myles ruminates as if explaining himself to his newest acquisition, "So you see, I've simply stopped giving them back. But here, you'll glow. Here, you, Tahseen, are immortal. Just like me."

Sparse light winks across the surface of the diamond that had been Tahseen. Myles, accepting this as all the affirmation he should ever need, winks back.

SHADOW GIRL

In the dark, everyone was beautiful. Everyone's kisses tasted of heresy and stolen wine, a magic carpet housed in the tip of every tongue. More affection and mercy seemed contained in darkness than in the cocks and tongues of her last twelve lovers combined. Nothing dispelled the flaws and shortcomings of weak but willing flesh so much as sightlessness; certainly not love, certainly not broken promises.

In blindness, everyone was beautiful.

Even her.

Tremaine's kisses, though sloppy and warm the way Josette liked to be kissed, always tasted ashen, always stank of cigarettes and gin. Tonight was a special night, however, and the only taste Josette found upon his tongue once she'd cuffed his wrists to the wrought-iron bedposts was her own. Tasting herself upon a man's lips and tongue tended to make her even greedier, even more feral than she typically acted during physical joinings. This, in invariable turn, tended to intimidate her lovers; shame them into the broken promises, the embarrassed shufflings of feet, the averted glances so damning by the overt glare of daylight.

So they'd attempt to recapture that pirated machismo through misogyny; pulling of hair, mauling of breasts, light smacks and hard ones. Or they'd seek exoneration for their failures of flesh and figurative bone through heartfelt claims that it had never happened before. All the more amusing when they did, was Josette's trust in the sincerity of every limp cock to share her bed. Whenever the words touched her ear, she knew that it really *hadn't* ever happened before, not before her, and that made it almost as funny as it was pitiable.

Almost.

Her teeth and fingernails could be cruel things at the height of her arousal, and this she knew well and took pride in. She had her appetites, just as men had theirs. Sharing blood would always be the most intimate and sensual kind of foreplay, no matter how many mothers' tongues clucked at the thought, no matter how many bibles were thumped in the name of a God who loves us enough to murder us at whim.

*****

Jefferson, affectionately remembered as her albino spider boy, and always dressed in perpetual white, was her first lover ever to call her pussy her "cunt." He seemed to hold far more fondness for it than for her as a sentient entity, often spending hours staring into its peony-colored petals in lieu of penetration. The notion amused Josette to such a degree that her laughter during sexual encounters was always frequent and usually uncontrollable. Aside from the occasional audience with that languid cyclops he called a cock, there was precious little to desire of him as a person. Jefferson, pale stick-boy with the almost too-delicately crafted cheekbones was also the first man ever to cry beneath her as she sank her teeth below his waist and sucked him bloody.

"Do you love me?" she would ask them from time to time after hours of spirited fucking in some dark place or another. Some of them, still gasping, still rigored and spasming with the melting bliss of ejaculation, would answer "Yes. Yes, I love you."

"Pity," she would reply.

*****

Cade, violin-voiced and breathtaking, used to sing to her as they clutched each other in shadow-crowded spaces under bridges. She'd wear velvet because he liked the sound it made when torn, and he'd wear the black leather choker she kept in her panty drawer for him; the one inscribed with the word "Broken." He'd hurl himself inside her, his cock stabbing deep with the ravenous fury of a striking snake, and Josette would squeeze him between her thighs until his seed overflowed her. Sometimes afterward, more than an hour would pass before they spoke, which was always fine with her. True intimacy did not necessarily go along with being inside her any more than a man's mere act of pressing together his palms signified that he was praying.

*****

Less than ten minutes remained before midnight. The time had arrived for Josette to join her beloved; to make Tremaine hers forever. She would cherish him all the nights of their life together, and perhaps in time, he would grasp the depth of her devotion. Not tonight, certainly, and perhaps not tomorrow night; but certainly in time.

*****

Galen, if she was to believe this was his real name, struck Josette as a lace-draped asshole from the instant they met. Even now, months later, revulsion coursed through her whenever a memory surfaced of his sweaty, unkind hands upon her. Here was yet another skinny, shaven-headed man-boy seeking to compensate for a lacking personality with pompous aggression in the sack. There were nights when he was tolerable purely for the unwitting comedy contained in the orders he would bark at her. "Turn the fuck over, bitch!" and "Scream for me, you little slut!" numbered among Josette's personal favorites. She'd spent the major portion of their final evening together teaching the asshole that such phrases, although perfectly suited to smut mag fiction, were less often as appreciated by live bedmates as by the characters in those stories, which were probably as much exposure as he'd had to sexual situations. Before that night was concluded, her bedsheets had come away from the mattress sodden with more of his blood than his semen, and it was Galen who'd learned what screaming was all about.

*****

Tremaine, much like this night, belonged to her. Tonight she could at last lay all the hurt and rage to rest. Damn the Jeffersons and Cades and Galens of the world. Damn all the others before them who'd found more to desire in the moist tightness between her thighs and asscheeks than in her eyes or words. Tremaine loved her, and that love was her sustenance and fortune and haven; all the things she wished to be for him as well.

"Happy Anniversary, my love," she told Tremaine, joining him in her bedroom. From a bedside wall sconce, the light of a single candle flared in the lightless room, playing deliciously over the honeyed brownness of her blindfolded fiancé's skin.

From the inky blackness of the room, his whisper greeted her, "I love you."

Nudging his blindfold up, freeing his eyes, Josette climbed astride her lover, mussing the short black braids crowning his head, and whispered, "Look at me, baby."

Tremaine obliged her gladly, filling his eyes with her; his fiancée, his world smooth and naked, firm and shaven and utterly his. The candlelight flickered over the tousled darkness of her hair, lending her curls a seductive sheen.

"I love you, Tremaine, and I want to be the best wife I can be for you. There's something I want you to know and believe always, angel. I want you to trust me on it, all right?"

"All right, love." His response came without hesitation, without the slightest hint of apprehension present to weight his voice, and Josette knew in that instant that she'd chosen wisely.

At last.

Josette replaced the blindfold. And kissed her lover's lips before fastening a red rubber ball into place between his teeth, and buckling its attached leather straps securely around his head.

"Love sometimes hurts, but all pain is fleeting," Josette told him as she stroked his eyelids tenderly.

Then she stabbed her thumbs down into his eyes, mired them savagely into the hot, snug space between orbital and eyelid. Tremaine twisted and fishtailed around on the bed, but Josette's thighs held firmly to him. Her thumbnails sliced the soft white meat of each eye, wriggled obscenely, stirring the blood and tears and viscera into a warm, red paste that glistened grotesquely by the light of the solitary candle. The sound that accompanied the act was a terrible one; the sound of angry needle-sharp teeth tearing into a hunk of spoiled meat, the sound of a thousand heads being wrenched from a thousand bodies in bloody unison. Then there was the screaming, which would cease no time soon.

“I love you, Tremaine,” Josette whispered against his straining, shuddering cheek. He shrieked up at her, spraying spittle, and Josette’s heart cringed. She’d confused him with this ultimate act of need and affection. She did love Tremaine from skin to core; loved him too much to bear the thought of his having to watch her grow older as they passed the years as man and wife. It was important to Josette that his last sight in life be one of her, youthful and vibrant, naked and affectionate and wanting him. Nothing masked the unwarranted assaults that aging wreaked upon the physical form so effectively as blindness. Nothing muted graying hair and softening breasts and slackening of the skin the way sightlessness would.

In the dark, everyone was ageless.

Even her.

HARD CANDY FOR THE DYING

Aric watched his lover smile at Trent as their fingertips brushed; a moist, lipless kiss of longing flesh. Their fingertips were fucking, goddamn it, and doing so in plain view. Did Marco think he wouldn't notice? That both Marco and Trent had chosen that precise moment to reach for the last beer on the table seemed less than accidental, so Aric waited for the sleep of thirteen hours on the road to seclusion to take hold of Marco before he cut Trent's throat. He did it with the paring knife they'd used earlier to carve liquor wells into blood oranges.

*****

The aged boathouse that shared the vacation property embodied death in a way that made it seem an attractive place to kill a man and dump his body afterward. White paint flakes like eczema peeled away from the bleached timber. Even in daylight, it looked like the rotting corpse of a larger, grander structure dead from neglect. Perched on stilts amidst the idyllic lake and verdant shore, it was an aesthetic affront; a cum stain upon green silk.

Aric went there whenever he could to smoke weed and scrawl lyrics to songs he'd never sing along its inner walls. He never wrote songs on paper, and never composed music anymore. The idea of strangers happening upon the lyrics, not knowing by whose hand they'd been rendered, or to what melody they might be sung was too entertaining for him to take the guesswork out of things. Aric thought it lent the shack kind of a Charles Manson vibe.

Trent had leaped at his invitation to view its interior.

The haphazard slash he'd opened while Trent stood reading the meandering veins of lettering smiled up at Aric, a red-black grin ripped in the tanned perfection of Trent's throat. Aric smiled back, pleased with himself for having taken something beautiful in his hands and marred it irreparably. Hell if the peroxide blonde on the dusty floor was going to jeopardize the relationship that Aric and Marco had hoped to mend by driving way out to the middle of fucking nowhere for a few days of solitude. No chance of him interfering now.

In the morning, he'd tell Marco that the hitchhiker they'd picked up twenty-odd miles down the Interstate had departed their lakefront vacation cabin unexpectedly during the night. Marco would buy that because Trent had spoken over dinner of how wanderlust lived in his blood. Aric knew it did, because he'd tasted it.

"I'm glad you're dead," Aric told Trent, bending close enough to the dead man's lips to inhale Stolichnaya fumes. No one gave a damn about a missing hitchhiker. Hell, who was around to even *know* he was missing?

The edges of the tear in Trent's throat pursed and spasmed. Blood like ink foamed forth, red-black bubbles like tiny thunderheads bursting in the balmy night.

More, Trent gurgled through the slit pulp of his handsome throat.

Aric gaped at him. Aric reeled on evaporating legs. What had he heard? What the fuck had he just heard? It couldn't be happening again! Not again. . .

Murder me again, Trent's gashed throat demanded, speaking to Aric as clearly and certainly as would a living Trent's lips have spoken. Corpulent blood jewels slid down Trent's neck. Was the wound weeping? Was it still a wound at all? Or was it a second voracious mouth salivating with some nightmarish need that Aric was better off not knowing about?

Aric flung his back against the boathouse's only door. He denied the obvious because to accept it meant to grant immortality to the only lover he'd ever allowed to dominate him. Instead, he searched his memory for the cause of such an hallucination as he'd obviously just suffered. He hadn't done anything stronger than weed in nearly four months, not since

Marco's last threat to leave his sorry ass if he didn't straighten up and resume taking the pills his doctor prescribed. *Pills, shmills.* Aric distrusted the fucking things. Last thing he needed on top of all life's other kicks to his groin was some damned prescription drug addiction.

"Impossible," he whispered to the rising dead man with the vacant eyes and smiling throat wound. Impossible, that voice instantly recognizable. Impossible, that arterial grin painting Trent's tee shirt and the edges of Aric's field of vision in venous ash-red hues. But Aric knew better than to ignore the vengeful spirit wearing Trent's body. As cruel a piece of shit as Guy had been in life, it was nothing compared to what he'd become since the last night he and Aric ever spent together.

Murder me like you did before, Trent's corpse whispered again though its neck, *You want to. Your doctor's pills can't stop you from wanting to.*

"Go away," Aric whined, flattening himself against the creaky boathouse door. He would have run, but didn't dare turn his back on the gruesome effigy with the lolling head, "I didn't murder anyone! I didn't murder *anyone*!"

You killed me, Gorgeous. . .abandoned me, Guy wheezed from the depth of Trent's throat.

"I . . .you know, you left me no. . ." Aric fumbled, searching for words he'd rehearsed a thousand times on a thousand morning-afters. "I had to. . ." Lecherous silence born of unresolved guilt shoved the remainder of the sentence back down his throat, crowding its way into Aric's mouth like an unwanted cock.

*Kill me again, Gorgeous. . .*the throat slash keened, the words mutating from plea to directive. Aric was not being asked, but commanded to once again kill the lover whom his leaving had driven to suicide.

That more than two years had passed without anyone calling Aric "Gorgeous" hadn't troubled him before tonight. Hearing it now tore open old hurts as if the word were a fishhook digging into burnt-flesh memories. His cock recalled the arctic lovebite of razor blades and barbed wire, the smirking mouth that embodied passionate malice on the best of nights. Aric squeezed his eyes shut, mashed his temples with his fists as if the sight and sound of his former master could be pressed from his head like so much water from a sponge. It didn't work.

Maybe this time, I'll stay dead. Guy's voice carried the same cutting amusement it had on that night he'd tethered Aric to their bed and left him to the naked, knife-wielding mercies of two sisters, twins that shared Guy's blood fetish. Guy had spent hours watching them fuck before joining them. Aric would not soon forget the frenetic roll of each woman's eyes as she straddled his body and Guy worshipped each sister's altar of flesh with his beautiful cock.

Why couldn't Guy be killed? Why didn't he ever stay dead? Could there be a grain of truth to that shit he always talked about the symbol tattooed across the expanse of his back? He claimed it granted him everlasting life. That he believed himself to be soulless was something he told Aric in confidence the first night they met. Aric believed him to be full of shit, just another brooding Robert Smith wannabe Goth boy raging privately again a world too secular to appreciate his dark genius. Aric met the news that Guy had taken his own life with grief, but also with a subtle sense of vindication that shamed him.

Yet here Guy stood, wearing a different face, but the latest in the series of pirated identities he'd assumed since dying to escape the agony of losing Aric to younger, Latin-sexy Marco. And Aric wanted Guy back. About this, there was no confusion, and this was cause enough for Aric to wonder what sorcery may have slept inside Guy, inked into his skin, at the moment of his death.

Trent's hands hung impotent at his sides as he rose to his full height. Blood like Merlot pooled about his feet. Aric considered the hands, wondered what mastery of tortured pleasures they held or didn't. For all his shortcomings, Guy's hard hands remained something about him that Aric still missed on occasion. Hands like feeding entities gorging on blood-smacked flesh. Hands that always found Aric's limits and shattered them without apology and smacked him across the face with his brokenness.

Come die a little, Gorgeous, whispered the demon in the dead hitchhiker's throat, *Become. I'll still respect you in the morning.*

Guy's tone mocked, albeit not without that infuriating mote of sincerity that typically underscored his wryness. Caustic though he was, Guy's affection was never suspect, and this was the shackle that had kept Aric at his side for so long. Carnivorous, the blades that carved trails down his cheeks for tears to follow, but Guy always soothed him. Guy always dressed the wounds, stitched the gashes, sucked the panic from Aric's lips. And in those days, Aric was contented to be broken a thousand times upon loveless razors that fucked with precision and bone handles, so long as it was Guy who always pieced him back together.

Come here, Gorgeous, and kiss me and kill me, Guy whispered through the throat of the dead man.

Aric's luck would not hold. Sooner or later, they'd find out what he'd done, and would come for him. The police, they'd find out about the dead taxi driver in his basement freezer back home, the guy who always sang to him with Guy's voice as he drove. They might even locate the head of that tattoo artist who handed out flyers on Mott Street while wearing Guy's face. He'd hidden that one in a special place, but it was merely a matter of time before they found that one as well. Then they'd realize just how busy Aric had been over the twenty-nine months, six weeks, and eighteen days since Guy packed his head with angel dust and crawled into a whiskey bottle to die. They'd snap their cuffs on him and pat him on his head and remind him that society's got laws, and that one such law states one mustn't go about slaying innocents just because one's dead lover may have taken up residence behind their smiles.

Fuck them, Aric would think as they strapped him into his government-funded sanitarium bed. Fuck them and fuck their laws and fistfuck the ten daily milligrams of FDA-approved escapist's denial he was supposed to swallow. Once reason divorced logic, once the laws of probability and reality toppled and fled underground, why should the laws of men be spared? All the chalky little antipsychotics in the world wouldn't help piece him together again. To expect that they should was purest arrogance, both on his part, and on that of the psychiatrist who'd prescribed the medication to help Aric through the psychotic episodes to which he remained so susceptible, even after nearly two years of treatment.

Dead men roamed the abysmal darkness of this night in search of rekindled love. *That* was the law, the only one worth Aric's adherence. Regardless of all that distinguished lucidity from dementia, surely the affirmations of his own senses could be trusted. Guy's voice invading his ears. The aroma of dead hitchhiker blood filling the poorly-ventilated boathouse and the deafening buzz of wading flies who'd begun stealing sips from its pool. It's cloying copper flavor weighting his tongue. If such palpable, definable entities as these were not to be believed, then truly, what was?

You know what you have to do, Aric heard Guy hiss.

The dead hitchhiker's head lolled atop a growing tumescence in the slashed throat. Aric watched without wanting to as the corpse tottered toward him. From the ruined pit of Trent's throat burst the tip of a plump, foraging penis. The pink-gray glans bulged from the slit shiny with blood and sanguineous ropes of mucus, stretching the wound wide. The slippery thing surged forth, a rippling riot of muscle that expertly mimicked guy's generous dimensions.

Become, Gorgeous. Do what you have to do, the dead throat commanded, *Do what you always do.*

Aric stood enchanted by the impossibly long phallus snaking from that dead wound in a lunatic's parody of a necktie. The blood-smeared creeping thing looked enough like Guy's member to warrant fascination as well as revulsion, and the joust between these two states accounted for but one internal conflict cementing Aric to the floorboards. How long had it been since he'd tasted his master's brutal hardness? How long since he'd ridden it to a tearful, shaming orgasm that left him shrieking hosannas to Guy's dominion over his flesh and spirit? In dreams bordering on nightmares, it rose nightly to wring pride from Aric's throat. Some night his ecstatic throes awakened Marco, whom he would lie to and then fuck until dawn to spend the sexual hunger inspired by those dreams. Some nights he longed for Marco to fuck him with razor blades strapped to his dick as Guy had and still did in dreams. Aric wanted it back.

Come into me, Gorgeous, Guy intimated from beyond the grave, *Become*.

When the dead man held out his unfeeling arms, Aric picked up the paring knife and took it all back. Just as he had with the tattoo artist and the frostbitten taxi driver. Just as he had with all who'd come before them.

*****

Aric wiped dead man's blood away from his eyelids and admired his handiwork with gobbets of viscera tangled into his hair. Smoothing his Trent-stained cock, he grinned at the cum-sodden corpse as if it could take note of the affection in his eyes, as if his staring long enough and smiling widely enough might earn him a smile in return. The paring knife dropped from his twitching hand, clattering to the sticky floorboards.

Trent's world lay opened to Aric, spattered across the floor and walls and ceiling in shades of red and pink and gray, but mainly red. Not until this moment had Aric realized just how many shades of red existed. These, even by the meager illumination of a single light bulb, were plainly visible to his eye. In fact, the reds were the only color Aric could presently perceive. Other hues, mattering no longer, had faded to such obscurity as to make them indistinguishable from one another. Only the redness, like beckoning flames that reduced the remainder of the world to a gray-black sea of inconsequential faces and locales, mattered. His blood fetish reawakened, Aric felt dominant. Rejuevenated. He felt alive again.

He had taken it all back. He had *become.*

Tonight his name was Garrick once again, no matter what his doctor told him, and the next time he and Marco made love would be classic romance. He smiled at the thought as he made his way through the gray night , a nude, beautiful beast dripping red life over gray grass, toward the gray cabin to gently fuck his sleeping lover from dreams. Their red feats of trust and stamina would recall nights of sacred ribaldry long lost to posterity.

Marco loved him, or believed he did. If this was truth, as Garrick believed it to be, then not only would Marco understand the new direction their relationship was about to take, but in time he too, would *become*. Time would surely tell.

Moonlight pooled in Marco's unseeing eyes where he lay nude and ravaged by tongue and cock and blade. A cloud of starving gnats roiled into the boathouse through its shattered windows and opened door, tracking the scent of blood. Their descent into his hair and nostrils went undisturbed. Washing their legs in the blood rimming the slit in his throat, they flitted about with a bearing that betrayed a sense of entitlement, gorging without a care.

Stepping into the cabin, Garrick spent several minutes seeking to account for the emptiness of the bed he'd planned to share with his lover. The sheets held no heat, indicating that Marco had not lain upon them in quite some time. Then Garrick remembered Marco coming down to the boathouse to look for him wearing Guy's face. He remembered this and veritably hurled himself out the cabin door and back down the slope he'd just taken, the one leading to the boathouse at the water's edge.

Everything he'd done was coming back to him. All of it. The last thing he remembered was Guy's voice inside his head, directing him to plunge that paring knife home over and over. He remembered obeying that voice, and how natural and familiar it had felt to do so. He remembered being unable to stop himself, even when Marco walked in on him, and Garrick screamed over the bodies of the two dead men in the boathouse. He screamed until sunlight rose to greet him.

Whether this new day would see Garrick resume his prescribed medication remained to be seen.

Time would surely tell.

STOLEN GLANCES

Jackson is fucking me again, having his way with the curvy quiet girl in the wire-rimmed glasses; fucking me tirelessly, the way a lover ought to. He fucks me every day, even though we're not lovers or really even friends; downstairs in the company spa, in closed board meetings, in my office with the door wide open. Jackson is inside me, stealing me, the conniving bastard. He's inside me fucking me with those eyes of his, orchestrating one anatomical mutiny after another in me. Making me as wet as a kiss. I want to fuck him too, almost as much as I want to gouge out his eyes. I'm nobody's whore.

I would scream at him to stop it, stop looking at me the way he does if I didn't know what perverse pleasure he derives from my unrest. I would demand, I would plead, I would threaten. I would swear to get even with him for the unwelcome moistness of my vulva, the cursed stiffness of my nipples if those acts would not serve merely to validate his emotional manipulation. He wants to break me. He believes he can and will have me willing and greased on my stomach, his vessel pleading to be filled. The man wants it so bad, even I can taste it. Jackson wants to screw me to my knees and have my thanks for the rough ride down. He wants me to swallow and smile and ask for seconds like the good little courtesan he's decided I have the potential to be, under his direction, of course.

Moments ago, he approached me with the news that today's stockholders' meeting would begin in five. Investors were already inside. I nearly groaned openly at the suggestion behind his eyes as he spoke; a mute invitation no less urgent for lack of voice. Standing there sipping coffee, he slid his phantom cock into me again, the imaginary cock that pushes deeper into my anus, my cunt, my throat with every second his eyes remain upon me.

Me, him, my bound wrists, my torn bra, his dark, groping hands, my shameful tears, his driving cock, my terrified cry as his hard brown hand swats my face, my bruised breasts and used, gaping sex, his cum overflowing my mouth, dripping from my chin, our shared orgasm; all of these and more lie behind that bottomless stare and eerily infantile grin. I fear them even as I hunger for them, and it's all his fault.

Understand. . .I don't simply mean that Jackson Banning has lustful eyes. What I mean to say is that when his eyes are upon me, I can *feel* them. I can feel his sight upon me, even (or especially) when my back is turned. I can feel his gaze move over my skin, warming me, kneading possessively like the hands of a sculptor molding warm wet clay into a thing to be prized by all. That gaze is a prison, a torturer's table, conflicting as an unwanted caress of tongues. One glance is all it takes. Before I know it, I'm so wet and full of rage that I'm shaking. Mutinous things, vaginas can be. How different would things be, had I been the one born with a cock?

The meeting has been under way for nearly a half hour. Discussion of fiscal planners and quarterly employee reviews is failing to distract me from Jackson's insistent stare nibbling at my breasts, the phantom fingers tickling my swollen vaginal lips. My nipples, stiff and no doubt visible now through my blouse, are throbbing. Of all days for me to come to work without a blazer. Bastard knows what he's doing. I could murder him for this.

I've barely begun speaking when I feel his phantom cock spear me uncomfortably in the ass. He fucks me like that for the duration of my presentation, sawing in and out of me with malevolent slowness. And to me falls the task of pretending everything is fine, that I'm not enduring the psychic bang of my life, not about to come down my leg for the invisible tongues lapping simultaneously at my clitoris, my breasts, my armpits.

Oh Jackson, you vicious asshole, you will pay for making me stammer, making me drop my portfolio on the floor in front of our investors. Oh, how you will pay. . .

The instant our board meeting adjourns, I lock myself into a ladies' washroom stall and stroke myself to a quick release. It isn't the first time I've masturbated on the job, nor is it the first time I've done it with Jackson's wretched face behind my eyelids, searing my mind.

Two weeks pass before my vindication, but the best-laid plans are rarely stumbled upon as arbitrarily as was mine. I have Jackson's wife to thank for the idea. She's lovely; a trim, model-pretty black woman in a business suit. Her fluffy tied-back braids bob as she strides toward her loving husband and his molesting eyes. Bitch will never know it was her visit to the office that inspired me.

Thirteen days after my embarrassing presentation, she visits Jackson on the job. She doesn't stay long, but I learn, from the exchange I overhear, that the missus is going out of town. She'll be gone six days on business. That's when I get the idea. My vengeance will not take that long to unfold.

*****

After work the next day, I rush home to change out of my office wear and into the strapless black velvet number I usually wear to pubs in order to get laid fast. I liberate my chestnut-colored hair from its jaded five-day-a-week ponytail mode, making a glossy veil of it that I am told perfectly frames my face. The shiny pumps I select to complete the ensemble have four-inch heels. Before leaving home, I remember to slip out of my panties. Inspecting myself in my rearview mirror as I drive to Jackson's home, I permit myself the slightest immodesty, wondering as I look myself over; who wouldn't want a piece of this?

Jackson doesn't answer his doorbell, so I hide myself among the shrubs outside his home for a little over one hour. It's a balmy evening, although I'd have wished for a chilly night. The cold could only serve to make me meaner. How dare the fucker keep me waiting!

When he finally arrives home, I venture from concealment and approach him. Instantly, his eyes are inside my dress, touching me, crowding into my tightest personal spaces. Jackson is no novice to contests of will and manipulation. Any other woman might fall for the utter shock with which he pretends to recoil as

I stride toward him. My dear Jackson. My lovely, twisted wretch.

The Derringer I lift out of my purse and press against his crotch swiftly lays to rest any notions he may have been harboring of continuing to play me for a fool. Or of sustaining his visual pity screw. I can smell his heat, his cologne. For the first time, it smells like fear.

"I have such an evening planned for us, darling," I whisper in his ear as he unlocks his door and obediently invites me and my Derringer inside with him.

*****

Several hours pass before I leave him without bothering to uncuff his wrists. Climbing into my car, I ponder the fun I've had this night with Jackson. I wonder whether he appreciates the amount of hard effort I put into ensuring that each of us got what we wanted tonight. I know from the way he pumps me with those eyes every day that Jackson's wish was to experience the slippery depths of my pink places, and so he did at my discretion. What I wanted was to fire the Derringer, and I did; squeezed one off beside his right ear in mid-orgasm. That was when he started to cry. As punishments for premature ejaculation go, having a gun fired beside one's face seems like such a trifle; a woman is capable of so many more creative methods of tormenting a poor lover. His tears amuse me even now.

I believe he found me intimidating. I believe he missed the loathsome fear always present in my eyes and body language whenever his eyes find me around the office. Tonight, I showed him a different woman. Thinly concealed were my hopes of encountering defiance as I put him through the rigorous paces of my mouth and sex, bursting his skin whenever possible. Perhaps the straight razor was a bit much. But then, who knew a torn scrotum would unleash so much blood?

The tiny crystal vial in which I collected Jackson's tears will stay close to me always. Upon arriving home, my first act is to wash his blood off of it. I string a sterling silver chain through its loop the way I have countless times before with countless vials containing the tears of other psychic molesters I've encountered in the past. Immeasurable is the sense of satisfaction afforded me by this newest addition to my jewelry collection. That brings the total number of tear vials I've collected from defeated sexual aggressors, to thirteen. One for every year since my abduction by a quintet of teenage boys whose gang initiation apparently stated that they had to not only rape a woman, but make her come hard against her will.

I wonder, from time to time, whether they ever think of me.

With this vial of his tears in hand, I now have a weapon; a talisman I might use to ward off his cruel visual urges. Should he return to work seeking to savage me psychically with that familiar lust clouding his eyes, he'll find me armored and ready, wearing this record of his pain between my breasts like armor, like a badge. My last thought before sleep claims me is of Jackson's hardness pressed between my vaginal lips as I straddled him earlier with my Derringer muzzle pressed against his sternum.

*****

The arresting officer's eyes are smoldering with lust as he and his fellows corner me at home. It is the morning after I visited Jackson, and the police are in my apartment, sent to collect me for questioning about the evening I shared with him. Their psychic tongues descend swiftly upon my most sensitive physical locales as they size me up, questioning me in turn. What's my full name? How long have I lived here? How long have I known Mr. Banning? Am I having an affair with him?

These men reek of repressed longing. It's on their faces, in the set of their mouths. Their policemen's sense of entitlement drives their every word and action as my rights are read to me. I can barely think, drunk with the sensation of their eyes moving so studiously over my curves and swellings. They want to fuck me. They want to rip my dress and take turns plumbing my tightness until I can't see straight. Between my thighs, I feel the savage friction of the arresting officer's intangible erection, the one he holsters behind those steely gray eyes, the one currently scrubbing my clit so fiercely that my knees nearly buckle.

When he cuffs me, I can feel his gaze loving me, stroking my neck. The young officer leading me out to the squad car is licking me with his stare, his gaze fixated on my breasts, and the tear vial bouncing between them.

Our progress leads us past my next-door neighbor, returning home from his morning stroll. He may be eighty, but his eyes upon my calves and hemline are enough to raise gooseflesh along my arms. I didn't realize that men his age still fancied such filthy sexual acts as suggested by the internal stirrings I feel as he watches me pass. Fingers. Cold. Slack-skinned. Methodical digits. Two? Three? Abusing my clitoris, making me slippery, tempting me to squeal with genuine passion.

When I bend to sit down in the police vehicle's caged back seat, the young officer assisting me doesn't waste a moment before lodging his huge imaginary member in me. I can feel his eyes at work, peeling away my clothes the way that his hands wish they could. I can't blame the man, I suppose. Who wouldn't want a piece of this?

COMING HOME AGAIN

At first glance, the broad, maize-colored disc of the moon resembled nothing so much as the admonishing eye of God, spilling turbid dissatisfaction on Nick's transgressions. As he stepped into the starless night, Nick made a mental footnote of being alone on the street. Shouldn't somebody be out? Visiting their friends? Delivering Chinese take-out? Racing home from work to the open arms of a husband or a wife, the open legs of a mistress?

Or those of a sister-in-law with a drug habit?

Sure, it was a shitty thing he'd done. Sure, a wife's pregnancy is no excuse for balling her twenty-year old cokehead sister, no matter how blonde said sister might be, no matter how fucking fantastic her rack is, no matter how willing she is to occasionally give up a little ass in exchange for money she'll doubtless use to buy more coke.

Nick lifted his eye to the window of the apartment he and Lisa had shared for the past eight years. Her riding him about his alleged "drinking problem" had ruined another evening. Was she still crying? Nick felt his heart sink within its bone cage. Never meant to hurt her. Deep inside her, beneath all the undeserved pain and sorrow he'd dealt her over the years, Nick hoped this knowledge remained; especially since Nick, cursed with his father's temper, was no more likely to change his spots than the old man had been.

Nick crossed the sterile avenue. A streetlamp spilled orange light in a fuzzy-edged pool on the beer-stained pavement. The traffic signal suspended above the intersection glowered at him through a singular crimson eye.

Virtual lightlessness ruled this place, save for that one functional streetlamp. Nick approached it with quickened steps that echoed in the dark. Again, his mind dismissed the absence of other human souls on the street with him. For whatever reason, his conscious mind insisted on evading the fact.

At the next corner, something bumped Nick's ankle as he passed beneath a streetlamp. He would have screamed without shame but for the knowledge that he'd require every bit of air in him, should he have to bolt, and screaming tended to squander that precious air. Afraid to move, afraid not to, Nick dropped his gaze to investigate. The vaguely spherical thing lying in his shadow was slightly larger than a grapefruit. Nick bent to examine the object, and came aware of eyes upon him. He felt them, although his observer remained unseen.

The object felt warm and slimy to his fingertips; must have rolled through something nasty in the gutter. Nick regretted touching it the instant he felt that spoiled-meat slickness against his palm. It tempted him to drop the slippery thing, but he'd already touched the disgusting mystery ball; might as well know what it was before he hurled it into the darkness. Nick pulled the thing into the orange light of the streetlamp, held it at eye level.

The skull was the size of a large grapefruit, like that of an infant. It felt oddly heavy in Nick's palm. Recognition broke slowly upon him, his mind recording and cataloguing each detail separately.

The eyeless miniature sockets like little windows through which rich, red meat could be seen. . .

Sometimes the senses were merciful that way.

The thinning, shiny slabs of blood-colored muscle stretched taut across its convexity. . .The smooth, toothless shelf of the upper jaw. . .

Sometimes they didn't deluge a person like water bursting a dam, flinging them beyond the safety of sanity in the blink of a blood-filled eye.

The rank, terrible odor that wafted from the spaces between its unsealed fontanelles. . .the yellowed shifting forms, like undercooked eggs visible in its brain vault. . .the way the thing yielded with decay beneath his hand, stuck in flaky, mucus-slick fragments to his fingertips. . .

The next instant found Nick hurling the ugly little thing to the ground and gurgling, gibbering in little trapped animal utterances; the sound of several screams of revulsion and fear and confusion all trying to escape a throat at once and getting tangled somewhere around the larynx.

Upon impact, the little skull morphed into a child's ball and bounced twice before rolling away toward the gutter.

Nick stared for a long moment. The hallucinations didn't usually come on until he'd had at least three vodka tonics.

Across the street stood a child in a pool of hazy orange lamplight. The sight of him instantly set Nick's already jangled nerves chiming again. Something about the kid seemed somehow wrong. The boy stood just a little too still for Nick's comfort, like a sculpture, like a mannequin. Watching Nick. He hadn't been standing there five seconds ago, Nick would swear to it.

He was dressed in a striped T-shirt the likes of those that Nick's mother used to put him in when he was a boy, and gray coveralls, sneakers, and a backward-turned baseball cap. The child could have been him, Nick mused, starting toward the child not so much because he wanted to, but because the little boy happened to be barring the way to the club that Nick wanted to visit. He wondered what in hell's name a kid that age was doing out alone at this time of night any damned way. The boy couldn't have been over five years old.

Nick bent along the way to retrieve the ball, figuring it probably belonged to the kid. The boy had not moved. He still stood where he was, a three-foot tall statue. All that was missing from that image were sheets of dried pigeon guano caked about the child's head and shoulders. Something was wrong here, sure as hell, but Nick couldn't seem to put his finger on it.

“This belong to you, kid?” he asked, offering the ball to the little boy, and softening his voice a bit, the way adults usually did when addressing little ones.

As he spoke, Nick consciously ignored the child’s strangely misaligned face. It looked swollen, yet mashed; the face of a prizefighter who’s taken so many hooks and uppercuts that the shape of his face has been permanently altered by the damage inflicted. His left eye was lost beneath the puffy, blackened folds of his swollen, blood-suffused eyelids. He breathed in shallow hisses, his lungs vibrating inside his little rib cage. His aspiration sounded phleghmy, like he was breathing through a partially submerged garden hose or sucking the dregs of an especially thick milkshake through a straw. Nick had heard this particular anomaly before.

Rales, more commonly referred to as “death rattle.”

The boy looked from Nick’s face to the ball and back again. He prayed the kid would just take it and go. Nick was still wrestling with an explanation for the fantastic hallucination he’d suffered minutes ago.

“Go on, kid, take it,” Nick told him, already losing patience. Something about the way the child was looking at him disconcerted Nick; like something smelled bad.

The boy said “It belongs more to you than to me. It’s your birthright,” and when he did, Nick noticed for the first time the bones sticking out of the kid’s throat. Dark blood welled around the places in his neck where they’d punched through the skin. Two wounds; each bone fragment protruding from the flesh for about half an inch. Not dramatically visible, but there, nonetheless. The kid was bad off, no doubt about that. The son of abusive parents, most likely.

But nobody could walk around with his cervical vertebrae jammed through his broken neck, could they?

“I don’t know what you’re talking about kid, but here,” Nick bent, placed the ball against the curb at the kid’s feet.

Nick started past the child, continuing on toward the club. He stopped, though; couldn't just leave a kid out here in the dark, especially one that was hurt.

"You have parents, son? Someone who looks after you, who might want to know where you are?"

"I am where you've sent me," the boy said, "where you'll be soon."

Nick couldn't imagine why the little bastard insisted on playing games with him. He'd give it one more try, and then to hell with this little mindbender, Nick was moving on to his destination.

Willing his voice steady, Nick said, "You're hurt, though. You look like you could use a little patch job." Nick tried to smile reassuringly.

The boy told Nick, "I'll miss me when you're gone."

That chilled Nick to the fucking marrow of his bones; something in the delivery, something that turned his belief in God on its ass. Suddenly, Nick felt more afraid for himself than for this boy, who all at once seemed capable of dealing with anything.

"Yeah, kid, whatever," he said, brushing past the child, hurrying on toward the club. There were drinks waiting there for him. He dared not look behind him for the remainder of his jaunt, and when he arrived, he was surprised to find himself out of breath.

But any forty-six year-old cigar-smoking alcoholic would be, having run the number of blocks Nick had.

*****

Nick tapped his cigar against the golden foil ashtray set before him. The column of soft gray ash at its tip crumbled, adding to the drifting dunes he'd been cultivating for the past three hours. The usual sedative effect of the thick Cuban stogies had yet to unleash their soothing sorcery. Into his fourth of the night, he still felt he could crush a throat just as readily as blink.

On stage, live and jaded nudes jiggled to a bawdy groove; all bass, no music. Underage runaways strutted their stuff, licked flavored gels from one another's pendulous breasts, writhed around on the laps of married men who believed it when the ladies said they loved them.

Nick dragged on his smoke where he sat watching a pretty goddamned spectacular brunette rodeo on the lap of a frat boy while his dorm brothers cheered. The kid's rolled-back pupils signified that this was the closest he'd ever been to a willing vagina. Nick allowed himself a wry chuckle, and took the remainder of his whiskey in a gulp.

When a soft hand came down on Nick's shoulder, Nick jerked involuntarily, scared beyond reason at the thought that the child had somehow found him. The ugly, terrifying little child with the face that looked like it had been through some kind of machine. . .

"Lap dance, sugar?"

"What?"

"I said I want to give you a lap dance, handsome."

She had to be twenty-two, twenty-three tops. Pretty thing, she was. The black girl standing behind Nick gave him that look topless dancers held in reserve for those clients whom it was suspected had come solely for the drinks.

As a younger man, Nick might have actually fallen to the width of her dark eyes, her taut, sweet-smelling skin, the luscious mouth all set to pinch into a demure little pout at the first hint of his refusal. *'I could have any man in the house,'* her look said, *'but I chose you, I want you. Come play with me before I change my mind.'*

Nick had seen the look a thousand times before on a thousand different faces. Hell, even on her face, directed toward other men on evenings when he'd come here in the past. All Nick saw on her face was *'Listen, I'll pretend I'm into you for a while if you'll give me some money.'*

And wasn't pretending what it was all about? Renting little fragments of one's deepest, darkest, wettest fantasies? Pretending that for one scant and golden instant, the world and all its pleasures are yours to command, that you sit at the helm of a universe guiding by your whims, steering events as you please, rather than merely flailing amidst the buffeting waves and squalls of a dubious existence, struggling every second to remain afloat and not drown?

"No thanks, sugar," Nick said. Despite his evening's harrowing beginning, he almost laughed when she gave him the pout on cue. She had the most attractive lips he'd seen in a while; delicately crafted for smiling and blowjobs, arguable though, though that order. Nick wondered how she had come to be here; looked too clean to be peddling ass so early in life.

"What's wrong, ain't I your type?" Her delivery dripped with coy implications of Nick's satisfaction should he allow himself to be swayed.

"Hell yeah, you're my type," Nick answered, deciding there was nothing to be gained by being rude to the woman. He couldn't fault her for trying to make a living. Hell, she couldn't be guilty of any worse crime than Nick himself.

"Well then?" she asked, crossing her arms over a set of breasts that belonged on a pedestal. Nick looked at them and wondered how the dancers kept their nipples erect all evening long without the aid of air-conditioning. The room was kept sweltering, so that each lady glistened with her own perspiration. It was cheaper, Nick imagined, than buying cases of sesame oil every few days.

"Well, how much would a guy like me have to pay to hold your attention a little while?" Nick asked. He was already well acquainted with the standard fee, but wanted to hear what she would tell him. If she were she thinking about ripping him off, then more might depend on this girl's answer than she could imagine. He heard her reply and decided that maybe they could help each other out after all.

"Where can we go to get some alone time?" He let his eyes spell it out for her, and a tiny part of him was delighted to see all the practiced gestures and phrases evaporate behind her eyes. She was about to break his heart.

"Oh, I'll make it worth your time. You just name your price, sweetheart," he added, watching her mouth open and lifting the hem of his tablecloth to reveal a wad of folded hundred dollar bills held together with a sterling silver money clip. It delighted Nick to see the faux ingénue evolve before his eyes into the savvy businesswoman he'd known her to be all along. Her doe-eyed coquette act hadn't fooled anyone and they both knew it. When she spoke again, her voice carried more professional amenity than it previously had.

"If you want to get cozy, we can get together in one of the V.I.P. suites. We'll have all the privacy we need," she whispered. Nick ground his cigar against the foil ashtray on his table and followed the stripper's nod toward the rear of the establishment where a stairwell would lead him to the subterranean V.I.P. suites known to all the club's patrons, but of which no one ever spoke. She turned and headed toward the rear of the room.

Nick finished his bourbon and made for the back of the room where she waited.

*****

Bloody darkness greeted Nick as he stepped through the rear of the room and found himself peering down a squat, carpeted staircase. The dancer stood below Nick at the first landing, bathed in seductive crimson light. To her right, the stairs continued downward, leading into more menacing darkness.

"This way to Heaven, sweetheart," she purred, "Don't keep me waiting. I need you." She turned on her toe so deliciously and continued down that Nick nearly screamed, and descended the steps after her. Heaven was a hell of a long way from where she was taking him.

Thoughts of burying himself in the dancer, rocking hard as he could against her ass propelled him. He sorely needed to work off a little frustration. If this didn't do it for him, there was always his adorable, doe-eyed little sister-in-law. Her door was but one thing belonging to her that was open all night.

At the first landing, Nick noted a wrongness growing in the air. His breathing was growing laborious. He didn't know whether it was his rush down the stairs that had winded him, or whether the darkness was to blame. Its disorienting effects stifled and were not lost on a mild claustrophobic like Nick. An even narrower hallway stretched away before him, more red light filling it. The dancer beckoned to him from the opposite end of the passage, then disappeared around a corner.

Drawing breath grew more difficult for Nick as he loped after her, literally snatching his every tattered, raggedy inhale from air that felt as if it was thickening. A metallic dampness permeated the space; the dankness of an abandoned castle's cellar, but without the drafts one would also expect. The sensation rivaled standing inside a tomb, a humidor, a mammoth vein. The scent like blood remained present, softly underscoring the warm air of the tube.

At the end of the hallway, Nick turned the corner just in time to watch his stripper disappear through a door signifying suite DD. His hope of escaping the sweltering funk of the tunnel evaporated as he closed the door behind him. No such luck. He still smelled it, stronger than before; an odd pheromone of blood and moist vagina. Instead of revulsion, Nick felt strangely stimulated, impossibly summoned and aroused and hungry.

She was there, shrouded in a canopy composed of organza or satin, lounging with crossed legs upon a circular sofa upholstered in what looked like leather. No other furniture occupied the space. The room had an odd shape; rounded, possessed of no discernible right angles, not quite circular, yet not quite oval. Deep red light seeped through the gauzy canopy like grenadine, like menstrual blood. In the tricky darkness, her eyes possessed a luminous quality that gave Nick only momentary pause. He'd had a lot to drink tonight and it was dark here; eyesight often lied under such conditions.

Nick's heart spasmed as he located a part in the canopy and slipped through it. He pressed his lips closed, swallowed hard as his mouth flooded with thick saliva. Nick unbuttoned his shirt with one hand, pulled it free of his pants with the other. In his haste, he tore two buttons from the garment without even noticing. The chest and shoulders beneath were worth a second look; not as lean as he'd been in his bachelor days, but impressive for a man his age. Normal white light would have revealed tight, fair, silvery curls of chest hair dusting him from the base of the throat to the rounded protuberance of his belly, but they looked blood-slick in this place.

The canopy curtains were pinched and bunched here and there in layers, woven-through here and there with meandering dark-colored cords that Nick could only assume were some sociopath's idea of clever decorating. If he didn't know better, the shiny, slimy-looking things could have passed for veins.

The stripper eyed him without moving. She seemed to want him on her plate. It turned Nick off. What the hell gave her the right to look at him that way, as if he were food? He suppressed his urge to drive his fist into her fine-boned little throat and instead opted to extend a few preliminary amenities. Maybe later, he'd reconsider that fist to the throat. Later, after he'd had his money's worth.

"What's your name, sugar?" he asked the whore in a guttural tone as she stroked him where it counted. She looked at him the same way the child had earlier this evening, and it was beginning to piss Nick off. He felt like they both knew something that Nick should know, but didn't.

The child. . .

"We don't use names, here, hon. You call me anything you want. I'm on your time now." Batting luxurious eyelashes, she reached into Nick's underwear and gave his manhood a squeeze. Her hand felt warm and tiny grasping his rigid shaft. Nick groaned, his erection tenting his boxers before it flopped free of them altogether.

The pretty stripper touched him again, slid his underwear to his ankles. Nick stepped out of them, watching her stroke him. Her wide eyes stared up into his like twin bullet wounds in that maddening red light. People tended to look hotter and hungrier, sexier, more urgent beneath this sort of illumination, and Nick supposed it had been chosen deliberately.

The temperature in the suite seemed to be increasing. Perspiration sprang forth at his forehead and armpits as the stripper's tongue flicked the aperture of Nick's cock. Her gentle bite pinched his helmet as Nick carefully took hold of her shoulders. Her fingernails gouged his asscheeks as the girl set to the task of swallowing his hardness. Lifting his cock, the stripper lapped at his balls, dragged her tongue along his length and thickness. For a time, happiness was the slurping sounds of his cock stuffing her throat, her bobbing breasts, the snug pocket of her sliding mouth. Soon Nick desired and took more.

Nick pushed the girl onto her back, watching her magnificent breasts rock as she went down. Her legs slid apart for Nick and as he propped himself above her, she gripped him by the shoulders, digging hard into his sticky flesh in anticipation of his penetration.

Each seemed to have the other right where they wanted them.

A sweat bead stung his left eye the instant he thought this, and he reflexively squeezed both eyes shut against the needling sensation. The stripper's soft chuckle enraged Nick. He'd have struck her if he could have seen her. Recognizing futility in his attempt at massaging away the pain, Nick opened his eyes.

And found himself alone.

No tender young stripper to be found lying beneath him, gazing lovingly up at him in her practiced manner. No firm breasts, or long legs to drape the smothering blanket of his body over. No one but naked Nick propped against an empty lounger with his pants around his ankles, and his manhood dangling, all dressed down with no place to go.

Risking a step backward as he searched the lowlit suite, Nick forgot that both ankles were still entangled in the pants wadded at his feet. The clumsy pirouette that resulted threw him to the floor, his naked buttocks coming down in something slimy.

Scrambling to his knees, kicking out of his pants, Nick let out an involuntary cry as his right hand punched through the satin covering the floor and slid over something beneath it that felt like a slab of warm, uncooked liver. The slimy patches glistened wetly like a pair of abrasion wounds in a child's skin. That feeling of some monumental wrongness afoot in his universe returned to Nick.

Nick fought to gain his footing. His unsteady feet tangled, sending him down again, flinging him forward through the canopy and onto the slick mattress. His second tumble rent another wound in the satin floor covering which was steadily darkening around the two tears he'd made in it, as if some fluid was soaking into the fabric, staining indelibly, like blood.

Nick clutched at the layered veils forming the canopy enclosure. The sheers slipped from his grasp, feeling mucus-slick, too slippery to be held. Nick's his fingers came away wet from the gossamer material, streaked with something he could neither name nor recognize in the sanguineous light.

It was then that an unexpected wave of sound crackled through every nerve in his body, seeming to come from nowhere and everywhere. It knocked him flat on his ass, summoned scalding tears to his eyes.

There was a distorted quality to the din, the sound of an audio cassette player with failing batteries. Long before the first one subsided, another excruciating sensory overload struck Nick, dancing through his synapses like a fatal dose of electricity. He fell to his knees, clutching his head, and made a tight fetal curl of his body in that tiny suite that seemed to be getting smaller as the volume grew. The terrible, muffled sounds kept coming.

To Nick's ear, they sounded vaguely like voices; voices that Nick perhaps should have recognized, but didn't. He wailed like a newborn when another siege assaulted him. And another. The sounds seemed to be straightening themselves out, growing clearer. Nick heard something that could possibly have been "I don't have to take this," and cringed as remembrance washed over him.

"I don't have to take this. . ."

He'd spoken those words earlier this evening. . .

"You hear me? I'm not taking any more of this until you start recognizing your sister for what she is. . ."

Screamed them was more like it. Screamed them at the top of his voice not twelve inches from his wife's nose. . .

"Nick, don't you walk away from me, we're not finished yet. . ."

"It takes two, babe, don't think I'm going to take the fall alone for this. . ."

"I can't believe you. . .what kind of man shifts the blame to an innocent girl, huh? She's only twenty-two years old for God's sake. . ."

"Well, she's the oldest goddamned twenty-two I've ever seen. . . and a cock tease, besides. . .but that's your *family, sweetheart! Yours! Go take it up with her. . ."*

"I'm taking it up with you, Nick!. . ."

"Like hell, you will. . ."

"And don't you dare think the fact that you were drinking at the time is going to make it any better. . .it makes it worse is what it does. . ."

"You know, dearest, you're really starting to piss me off. . ."

"Damn it, let go of me! Stop it, Nick, don't. . ."

"Shut up, all right? Just shut your fucking mouth. . .you started this, so don't go all pissy on me now. . ."

"Nick, I said let go!. . ."

She'd groaned then, a sound that stabbed Nick's heart like a white hot javelin now as he recalled his rough hands tightening around her wrists. At the time, the only emotion he'd been capable of feeling had been rage; rage for her forcing him to behave in such manner. Hearing the sound again, remorse flooded into his heart like rainwater into the crawlspace beneath a rotted house.

He'd released her wrists when she cried out, but only to shove her away so roughly that Nick's pregnant wife was sent into a sprawling spiral that landed her on a sofa hard enough to drive the wind from her lungs. He'd immediately stepped up to shake her hard by the shoulders, and Lisa had responded to this by digging her fingernails into the meaty part of Nick's forearms. That was one thing about Lisa; she would never curl up in a corner and cower before an angry husband. Nick supposed he'd sustained more scars tangling with her than he had in twenty years of bar fights, and his wife never seemed to suffer from the fact that her husband had a nearly seventy pound weight advantage over her. Ordinarily, Nick admired that spirit, but tonight had been different. He'd already had a few drinks by the time they argued, and his reward for finally returning home after three days must have been that his inebriation cushioned Lisa's blows, for he hardly felt a thing as they wrestled. He'd given her one across the face, just to spite her ripping up his forearms, and a rosy bruise blossomed almost instantly on her fair skin.

That was one of the things that had first drawn Nick to Lisa, her fair skin.

It was when she landed a lucky kick—a cheap shot, a sucker's feint—to the balls, that Nick's fury had overflowed and his jaw had tightened, and he'd clenched his fist and driven it home as hard as he could. That would show the bitch.

Nick lay curled on the floor of the canopied platform, his head resting upon a puckering mass of fleshy, shining material. Something resembling viscera plastered to his forehead. Nick could hear his heartbeat thrum through the air, shaking the very room. He assumed it was his heart, after all, who else's could it be?

Lisa's cry rang out like the report of a firearm as Nick's fist connected with the fleshy dome of her stomach. Just as suddenly as the scream was there, it was gone, as if she'd given up on it in mid-wail, as if no amount of screaming could adequately relieve or express the magnitude of the pain radiating through her mid-section. Or as if she wouldn't give Nick the satisfaction of hearing her torment. Nick stood over her a moment longer, grappling with something he wasn't even sure he'd heard. A sound, faint, almost inaudible. It had been there, hadn't it? An instant before he'd buried his fist in her belly, the sound had been there. He'd heard it as surely as he breathed. It had been a scream, a terrified little scream, the voice of an insect screaming his name, and it had come from inside Lisa's abdomen, from her womb. . .

Dripping with perspiration, Nick shivered now with his memory of earlier deeds. On his side, trembling beneath angry red illumination, he heard the sounds and relived the hell of the struggle he'd had with his wife hours earlier. He heard her shrieking in pain as they assaulted each other, and the room seemed to reel this way and that. He remembered striking Lisa across the face, remembered the sight of her porcelain cheek flaring as if purple ink had been splashed across it. Nick remembered being disgusted by the sight of her. . .bitch. . .unfair bitch. . .hateful judging bitch. . .

He remembered curling his fist so tightly that it ached for an instant, and then pushing it forward into. . .

Nick leapt to his feet, his left nearly going out from under him as his arms windmilled, as he tried to steady himself. The room had definitely grown smaller. Despite the impossibility of it, the distance between walls that earlier had stood a fair fifteen feet apart now barely exceeded Nick's armspan. And where the hell had the door gone? Whirling in search of it, he found nothing. Nick was trapped without a way to get himself out or to summon help inside.

All at once, he was terrified. All at once, he knew what the next few seconds held for him. He grabbed at the visceral canopy veils and almost went down before regaining his footing. Nearly all of the satin that covered the floor was either gone to tatters, or soaked with blood. His wife's blood. . .

Oh God, no. . .No God, he thought as he stood waiting for his theory to prove itself or to fail and deliver him from. . .

Nick filled his lungs with that syrup-thick, clotting air, and shouted at the height of his voice, knowing that if he was not heard in this solitary shot at survival, he was as good as dead.

The voice that tore out of him sounded ragged and unfamiliar as he shouted “No! No, Nick don’t, Jesus, don’t!—”

Glaring at Lisa, ignoring the dull ache in his sliced-open forearms, ignoring a scream from within her that he wasn’t even sure he’d heard, Nick sent his huge fist, hurtling forward at an uncanny speed, pushing hard into the protuberant tenderness of Lisa’s swollen belly, far too angry to consider that to do so, was to kill the life-force within.

Nick experienced only a moment of fear and pain as the canopy layers he faced imploded toward him, standing naked there in his room with its visceral floor and walls so red and warm, so much like a womb. He stood there and cried beneath the titty bar wherein he’d cheated on his wife too many times to count.

In his last instant of conscious, living thought, Nick remembered the strange child with the ruined face that he’d met earlier, and the decomposing little skull that he’d found on his way to the club. Images raced along the interior of his skull like rapidly flipped pages in the book of his life, there and then gone. What Nick recalled most of all, was Lisa the way she was when they’d first met, the perfumed smoothness of her skin.

He had just enough time as he stood there beneath that visceral canopy formed by Lisa’s amniotic sac, to regret everything he’d put her through, every tear she’d ever shed because of him. Then the suicidal fist came smashing into his pregnant wife’s stomach, making Nick, much like their unborn child, a memory.

SHE WAS VOLUPTUOUS ANTIQUITY

She seems as much derived from the word "fanatic" as does the term "fan" itself. Ariadne. My self-proclaimed number one fan. Her matted lime-colored dreadlocks bounce and sway with her step like a crown of restless adders. A skillfully rendered blacksnake is inked into the left leg of her blue denim lowriders. The white V-neck beneath her black Eddie Bauer stretches the word "Lovechild" across her breasts in blood red ink.

She stalks toward the corner table I always claim at these monthly erotica writers' gatherings, the one farthest away from the overhead lamps. Her stride bears a languid just-out-of-bed gait that seduces willfully. The unsubtle interest lifting the eyebrows and turning the heads of every man and woman she passes suggests she'll not be returning to bed alone tonight if she doesn't want to.

"Tattooed freak with a goatee?" she asks me, reciting the closing signature I usually employ in correspondences with her. It seemed the most recognizable self-portrait I could offer to this fan of mine to whom I have written for nearly a year. I nod, getting to my feet, as her smile becomes a grin. I inherit the envy of the room when we kiss hello.

"Gorgon girl with hands of ice," she replies, citing the signature she always leaves at the bottoms of her letters to me. Her voice is a phantom serpent winding leisurely about its prey. She fingers a single Medusa-esque lock of her hair and seizes my offered hand in a grip so cold that it seems bloodless.

"It's good to finally taste you," she sighs, seating herself across the gin-sticky table from me. A waitress appears at our tableside, solemnly removing the ashtray I've filled with ganja-laced butts. Ariadne orders a tequila sunrise. I stick with my good friend, Jack Daniels, straight up.

The tavern is hugging a full crowd tonight; haven't seen this many new faces at a writer's gathering in ages. Our drinks take nearly fifteen minutes to reach the table, and when they do, they're mostly ice. We spend that time discussing my writing efforts and hers. Ariadne is a fiercely erotic poet of whose musings I am gratefully enamored.

"Your writing resonates," I confess to her between sips of Jack, "You have a breathtaking talent for painting with words." Never in my adult life have I used the word "breathtaking" conversationally. I realize I must be drunk. It amuses me all to hell, which is another betrayal of my inebriation. Everything is funny when I'm drunk.

"Not like yours does," she counters, "Your language. . .it stirs something . . .wanton in me. It liberates something in me that I can't quite name."

"I do look to have my own voice when I write. I think most people do."

It's nearly eleven p.m. and I've been sipping Jack Daniels since half past six. Convinced of my immortality, I tell Ariadne, "Thanks for coming tonight. Your compliments are proving to be almost as sweet as your lips." It sounds saccharine and insincere, but it sets her smiling at me again.

Liquid courage. Gotta love it.

"I believe women write erotica to take control over their fantasies," she follows up, "We write erotica to explore our wildest imaginings from safe distance. After all, it's fiction; no author has to suffer any real-life consequences that taking a more active hand in that kind of exploration would invite."

Her lips inflame me. "And men's motives? Are they as introspective?" I ask.

"Men write erotica hoping to get laid. Most of you. They write looking to get laid by women who write erotica, or who at least read it. Anyone claiming otherwise is full of shit." She drains her bloody-looking cocktail as if to emphasize that declaration, and lights a cigarette.

I can't suppress a smile at Ariadne's conviction toward this rationale. Against my will, my eyes leap across the tavern to where a malevolently fuckable author named Moon Lustgart stands sipping martinis. Moon and I spent most of last year's Annual Terrorscribe Conference naked in my hotel bed, sweating into each other's eyes and mouths.

Didn't go there looking to get laid, however that hope *does* accompany me to every one of these monthly meetings. Wonder what that says about me.

You want wild imaginings? I muse privately as her statement about women who write erotica resurfaces in my head. Feeling further aroused by the memory of moon's mouth working below my waist than I already was, I think, *Oh, the things I could show you. . .*

"Then thank God I don't write erotica. I write *erotic horror*. Different beast altogether."

Her laughter is grudging. "Naturally. I forgot you're the exception to that rule. I'd go so far as to say you're probably the exception to every rule there is."

"Damn right." We're both laughing now; cackling like a couple of lushes. I haven't laughed this hard since before my wife left me. I've missed it.

"Do you want some of this?" she asks me, casting eyes as green as jade marbles downward in invitation for me to follow her gaze. I spend several seconds admiring her generous chasm of cleavage before realizing her question applied to the cigarette she's offering. Embarrassment sets fire to my face and throat as I sit praying my confusion will go unnoticed.

"Or would you rather have some of this?" she teases, lifting the cigarette to eye level, convicting my lecherous ass with an amused tilt of her head. As she smiles, it occurs to me that I'd really relish the opportunity to hear her come.

"I'd. . .Jesus, I–" What am I to tell her? That I'd really like to see her naked? That I'd give my right arm for one taste of her fucksweat? That I'd like to finger her until my wrist cramps?

Not entirely untrue, these; but monumentally inappropriate without a doubt.

She lets me off the hook mercifully. "Here. Smoke." I oblige her, having smoked my last before she arrived.

"So tell me about your week," I ask, "What'd you do last night?"

"Caught my Jazz with a Val and had to kick the Val's teeth out."

I understand the part about her kicking out someone's teeth, but the rest of it would be cryptic even if I were sober. My facial expression apparently betrays my ignorance, because she follows up with clarification.

"Jasmine. My girlfriend. Caught her in bed throating Val, my ex-fuck buddy and Yoga instructor. Kicked most of his teeth down his sorry-ass throat. The bright side is they're working real miracles in the field of cosmetic dentistry these days."

I'm unsure which unnerves me more: the admission, or the aplomb with which it's delivered.

"You kicked a man's teeth out, and New York's Snidest hasn't come to fit you for a pair of chic chained-together bracelets yet? Didn't Val press charges?"

"Not yet. But he will in another five minutes or so. I'm going to die in police custody tomorrow night," she says, checking her watch, "Right around this time."

"How do you know that?" I ask.

"Same way I know you once spent an absolutely exhausting night with an underage prostitute because you had an idea for a story on the subject, and you believe living out sordid experiences lends you credibility when you write on sordid topics."

Struck dumb, I can only stare, and wonder what else this woman knows about me that my wife doesn't. I resist the suspicion creeping like a leprous hand up my spine, whispering into my brain that extortion is her game.

"I also know you never wrote the story." She adds.

"Who the hell are you?" I ask, sobering quickly and unwillingly. It seems the only thing to say. And even as I lend voice to it, I trust a stupid question will yield a stupid answer. This, I trust because besides having to work very hard to keep from trembling, I find us holding hands even though I don't recall lacing my fingers with hers.

She tells me, "I'm your biggest fan."

"Well if you know you're going to die, why aren't you trying to circumvent it? Why aren't you sitting behind a pair of dark shades and a fake beard on a one-way jet to Canada? Or turning yourself in tonight, so that maybe–"

"Because there's no place for me in this world. I'm bored with it. I embrace what sleep is coming to me twenty-four hours from now."

Is she fucking with me? Testing me? Trying to get a rise?

"Why did you come here tonight?" I demand. I'm all for getting a little tight over some good conversation, but goddamn if I'll be toyed with.

"I want you to immortalize me. I want to be your most sordid story ever penned from actual experiences."

"And you want this done tonight?"

"Sure. It's my last night as a taxpayer," she tells me, "When's a better occasion to celebrate in such a way?"

"Yeah, but listen. . ."

She's on her feet already. "We'll go to my favorite place. I'd take you to my apartment, but the police are on their way there to rifle through my panty drawer as we speak."

I don't ask her how she knows. I simply follow her outside.

*****

I haven't scaled a fence since high school. Haven't scaled one while drunk in my entire life. Landing on my ass in the shrubbery framing these forbidden grounds, I remember why. Ariadne's progress over those iron fleur-de-lyses crowning the eight-foot barrier is as swift and feline as I'd imagined it would be. Obviously, this business of trespassing in private cathedral courtyards is not new to her.

The gothic monstrosity gleams in moonlight like a black ice carving. I swear I can hear the building breathing; can see its outer balustrades swell and fall with its aspiration. Cathedral or not, everything I'm sensing about these grounds tells me God's never come within a country mile of this place.

Dead vines like licorice ropes vein its cool surface. The black stone house regards us through unblinking stained glass eyes. Iron chrismons hang above its lintels, perch atop its peaks like suicidal divers preparing to take a final bow on their way down.

Ariadne leads me deeper into the courtyard, toward one of three low-hanging willows beneath which a backless granite bench squats. Her step is purposeful but unhurried, conveying all the quiet authority of an empress conducting a tour of her palatial estate.

The sway of her hips is firing me up. I want—no, I *need*—to fuck. She can see it my eyes as plainly as I'm reading it in hers. She needs to fuck too. It's why we're here.

"Help me live forever, angel," she tells me, unfastening my pants to stroke my genitals. My cock is a monolith as I push her jacket down her slender arms. Her mouth crushes cranberry-painted heat against mine.

Questions burn my mind as her hands of ice traverse the tattooed topography of my abdomen. Should I ask? Do I really want to know?

Radiance breathes tonight, and I have been pulled inside her. She is Gorgon Medusa, still turning men to stone. She is a naked daughter of myth to be rhythmically pressed in worship of elder goddesses. On my knees, I bow my reverent head and thrust forth my cock's sacred obelisk in offering. My tongue composes silent elegies to forgotten deities in its quest for her favor.

She's discovered the place behind my ear that when licked slowly, makes me dance inside my skin. Rising nipples strain at the front of her tee. I peel it off over her head, freeing them, and she's upon me. My back kisses dewy courtyard grass. I taste her skin, biting when her teeth savage me in intimate places. Her green curls writhe as if unseen hands are at play amid her locks.

My mouth crushes swollen lips as I whisper hosannas into her cunt. I am captured and lost in her maelstrom of flesh. I am the favored son of immortals. The oily sweat glossing her skin is my birthright. My unyielding supplicant is hers.

"We wear our serpents on the inside now," she hisses through spit-threaded lips, opening my back with fingernails like fangs. I can smell my blood, and it's making my mouth water.

Black vipers hiss mantras from the cathedral of her cunt and temple of her ass as my devotion fills her, throbbing. From within those holy depths, they uncurl. They snap at my erection, punch loving fangs through my scrotum while I dance against her, jubilant as a sinner saved.

Their venom anoints me.

*****

I've never been bitten by a snake. I won't pretend it doesn't hurt like a mad bastard. That act wouldn't fool a girl scout.

Can't get those glaring wounds out of my head. I counted as many as seventeen upon arriving home last night; seventeen snakebites savaging my abused cock, tearing my scrotum. Seventeen love bites ordaining me her priest, her disciple, the keeper of her legend. Then I abandoned counting for sleep. Being well-rested is essential, I think, if one hopes to ably approach the masochistic folly of composing remembrance for a goddess.

At my writing desk, sitting with my swollen, Bacitracin-smeared nuts resting on a towel filled with ice cubes, I lay down my pencil for the eighth time, and swear softly. It's nearly midnight, and more tears than words stain the page before me. I've been sitting here since nine o'clock this morning, and all I can show for evidence of that is a numbing ass, and an empty, acid-washed stomach.

It's eleven fifty-three p.m. I close my eyes and feel my heart break. The police have found her. I know Ariadne is dying, just as I know that black serpents are dancing between her smirking lips; just as I know that soon after I'm killed in an auto accident two years from tonight, I will meet her again; my Gorgon girl with hands of ice. Not in Heaven. Not in Hell. Someplace else. Someplace real and warm, where loving snakes abound.

Don't ask me how I know.

I just know.

Okay?

KEEPER

Panic.

Dry-mouthed, stammering, five-alarm panic, the fast, fatal kind that fills the bladder quickest has taken up residence beneath your skin, and finds you assaulted with sudden awareness of every bead of sweat gathering across your scalp and beneath your arms.

Panic has come home to your spine, worming between the vertebrae with all the subtlety of a hammer pounding railroad spikes into place. Why do you keep letting Spiro talk you into these two a.m. pub crawls? Has he ever failed to abandon you in favor of shadowing the most inebriated skirt in the house until she agrees to leave with him? Is tonight any different as you hug the bar with only your scotch and soda for company? Why do you keep letting your brother sucker you into this?

Because you're a damn barfly, and they keep the lighting low here at Doonan's, which could some night work to your advantage. Because you've gone six months untouched by any orgasm that didn't involve hand lotion and wrist cramps, that's why.

Panic, the mind-numbing sort, an anti-pheromone that hangs about you like some sort of social infirmity, has set your thoughts spiraling away, aimless as ashes scattered by a foul wind. You wonder if the hottie behind the bar notices this as she speaks the words to which your unrest is attributed.

She begins, "Hi. My name is—," but you've already stopped listening. She's that hot. Irish accents have always driven you wild.

Stop it. You're staring at her lips. Stop staring at her lips. Stop it stop it stop it. Stop staring at her fucking lips before your thoughts head south and—

. . .the fullness and contours of a woman's mouth are purported to represent a fair to exceptional mimicry of her vulva. . .

Isn't that what Spiro's always told you?

Jesus. . .Jesus Christ on a pony. . .

Her hair frames her face in corkscrew curls that look like heaven and probably feel like it when dragged gingerly along the stomach. Black Lycra top, lacy and sheer. A milky bead of moonstone like a splash of cum drips from the belly chain stealing your attention and holding it captive at her navel. Is that a miniskirt she's wearing above the ripped fishnet stockings? No, don't look, asshole! You keep your fucking eyes above her fucking chin, or so help me—

. . .black, hip-groping mini, twenty-percent cotton, forty percent poly, forty percent Lycra, judging by the breathing snugness of it. . .

She's talking to you. What did she say? What in Heaven's name is she talking about, and how long has she been going on about it? Don't know what's funnier: the fact that you're sitting here wondering what it'd be like to yodel into the shadowed chasm of her cleavage, or her genuine belief that you're paying attention to the conversation she thinks she's having with you. But you haven't the remotest idea of what the topic is, and you don't care, do you, you sweaty pig? You could almost believe in God again, just watching her form words with those glossy rosebud lips that'd probably feel so sweet whispering your name into your neck.

. . .neck neck neck whispering into your neck her neck her slender delicately crafted neck designed for languid nibbling. . .

Don't think about that. Her lips aren't anywhere near your neck and aren't likely to venture there. Ever. So quit thinking like a sex-deprived teenager, and for fuck's sake, get that imaginary tongue of yours out of her mouth. Order another bottle of Bud. Yeah, that's it.

"So what'll you have, love?" she asks, awaiting your drink request. Your ears haven't remembered how to hear yet.

Damn it, can't she quit being so goddamned fucking cute for five seconds while you get your bearings? Can't she?

She's laughing at something you just said. Don't expect anyone to believe you planned that. You're lucky your legs haven't given way beneath the bulk of your resounding social ineptitude. Maybe she has a thing for boyishly awkward bastards with bad skin and worse hair who get flatulent when they're as nervous as you are right now. Or maybe it's something simpler and easier to understand that's amusing her. Maybe there's a booger stuck to your eyebrow.

You can feel Spiro's eyes evaluating you as he wafts past your back, accompanying a pair of nearly naked blondes outside into a night sure to end with the ladies buried beneath a pile of spent condoms. The look in his eyes smacks you across the face. It warns you to do what he'd do, or suffer the caustic wrath of derision as only older brothers can deal it when you return home still celibate. His eyes find the face of the shapely bartender currently fetching your second drink of the night, and urge you to quit being a pussy and get her number.

Panic.

She's returning with the Campari and soda you only requested because you read in a magazine last week that bitters and soda would be this summer's "it" drink. She smiles at you as she sets it down. Whatever you've been saying to her seems to be working its mojo, because she's definitely into you. She wants to fuck you. How long has it been since you've been able to claim as much about anyone, save for the homosexual bodybuilder who lives two doors down from you?

Nothing left to do now except find out what time her shift ends, and wait around to talk her into coming to see your apartment.

And know panic over whether you've got the tool for the project ahead. Do you suppose yours will be the largest, finest cock ever glimpsed by a woman as mind-blowingly gorgeous and fuckable as she? Perhaps your four-and-three-quarter inches will deliver her best lay ever and she'll swear so with tears streaming from her afterglowing eyes? What have you allowed Spiro to trick you into, you fool?

You wonder whether that impotent muscle cowering between your thighs will shoulder its responsibilities nobly, or whether it will duck and cover the way you do every time life calls upon you to act decisively. Perhaps the universe will grant you a small mercy and simply have you go limp with sheer stage fright, rather than letting you vomit fear and foul liquor all over her tits the way you did with the last woman who almost laid you. Remember that?

Look at you. Now you're even panicking about panicking.

Damn Spiro. Does he ever go through this? Did he go through it the night some crazy, murderous bitch pushed a letter opener up his right nostril and into his brain? Was it this kind of performance anxiety that drove him to rape her in the first place?

No, not Spiro. Your big brother was no rapist. He may have gotten a little rough with the redhead he picked up in this very same bar five years ago. Perhaps she changed her mind once he got her alone with his surgical needles and rope-wrapped beer bottles and sandpaper. But he no more raped anyone than he proposed marriage. Spiro favored a touch of violence, a spot of the unorthodox when enjoying a conquest, because he knew most of them liked it that way, and those claiming otherwise were fun to convert. That's what he used to tell you whenever you came to him for advice on sexual things. "It's not memorable if it doesn't hurt," he used to say.

"So I was wondering," you finally muster the *cojones* to venture to the curly bartender, "Could we continue this conversation someplace else. . .once your shift is over?"

Her smile says it all. You're in. Wherever Spiro is, you know that he knows, and that he must be beaming. Tomorrow morning, he'll tell you he never doubted you for an instant, and that he always knew you had it in you, even if you didn't know it yourself. He'll admire your handiwork and supervise your disposal of the headless body in your guest bed; the bed with the plastic tarp beneath its sheets.

Make him proud.

He is, after all, your brother, and today is his birthday. His being dead doesn't change a thing with regard to that.

So remember your brother later as you finish ripping her strategically-torn fishnets. If not for Spiro, you wouldn't be where you are tonight; poised on the precipice of deviant godhood. And where your brother's carelessness snatched defeat from the jaws of victory, you will succeed, because you've always been the superior planner. There'll be no stories on tomorrow evening's news about a woman's narrow escape from the cradle of depraved misogyny that is the apartment you and your brother once shared. The loaded syringe beneath your mattress will ensure that she does not escape your staple gun, your soldering iron, your crushed glass offerings to her sensuality. Spiro will be so proud of you for honoring his memory in this way.

Now finish your drink and try not to fall all over yourself getting off your barstool. Must keep your façade intact long enough to get her to your place. Everything will be fine, so long as you don't panic.

Tonight promises to be. . .memorable.

SAVING EVAN

I remember the one time my roommate Evan raised his voice to me. Tonight, precisely one year after the occurrence, I can still distinctly recall every detail of that evening.

"What have you done? What in God's name have you done?" he'd shrieked.

In those days, the existence of God was a notion even more abstract to me than home-cooked meals or loving parents or hot showers with perfumed soaps, so I laughed at him. I laughed reflexively, used the still-smoking revolver at the end of my arm to wave him off, not knowing the reason for the terrified flaring of his nostrils.

I know now.

Sure as hell, I know now.

Describing Tasmin is difficult. One might as well attempt to gauge the color of love or the sound of fear. It is enough to say that a night does not pass that I don't dream of her and wake up screaming.

The word "Faceless" springs to mind as a fitting description for her. "Carnivorous" is another good one, I think. "Deceptive" also works.

The more thought I devote to the lady, the less difficult finding adjectives to ascribe to her becomes.

I suppose I can't say Tasmin never did anything for me. I do owe her a debt of gratitude for at least ridding her mouth of Evan's penis before greeting me for the first time. Mine had been the misfortune of walking unannounced into the bedroom I'd shared with him for three years.

To his credit, Evan had demonstrated decency enough to look sheepish upon my intrusion. After all, it was my bed they were using, despite the presence of Evan's less than five footfalls away.

"Pardon me," I'd offered once my shock and umbrage abated.

"You must be Aaron, the roommate," she'd said, her lips glistening grotesquely as she smiled up at me from where she knelt between my roommate's legs, "Under different circumstances, I'd kiss you hello, but I doubt you'd favor that right now."

She wasted not a moment in filling my shocked silence, adding "Or would you?"

I nearly screamed at them both. Evan looked so absurd lying there on my bed—on *my* bed, damn it!—with his jeans pushed to his ankles. I left the room without closing the door behind me and spent the afternoon at the movies. On my way out of the apartment, I made sure to pause in the kitchen long enough to eat the last slice of chocolate cheesecake out of the refrigerator. It's Evan's favorite.

"I have to know, Evan. Where did you find her?" I said to him that evening after she'd gone and I'd returned home.

"Her name is Tasmin. Picked her up at that rave you were too busy to go to with me last night," he replied, not looking up from his newspaper to meet my eye.

There was no misreading that wounded-kitten tone of voice. Had it been me and not him who'd been subjected to desertion at the altar by a fiancée of two years, then I too, would revel in company whenever I could find it. This would hold especially true, had my best friend chosen the last possible moment to break plans made days in advance, as I had done to him.

Hardly was I without my own problems, though. Sometimes I resented my friend for his neediness. Sometimes his behavior tempted me to remind him there are other unhappy people in the world who do just fine for themselves because they've got no choice. I certainly had no choice in being born addicted to heroin just like my dear sweet mother who'd started using at age fourteen and continued abusing us both throughout her pregnancy. I damned sure had no choice in the half dozen foster homes I passed through between ages nine and sixteen. And I fucking well didn't have a choice with regard to the nervous breakdown that took me at age twenty-two. I've never retreated from life the way Evan sometimes does, though. I've never willingly acted as a burden to those around me the way he sometimes does. Not for a moment.

Aware that no good would come of interrogating him about Tasmin, I left Evan to his reading.

"I'm sleeping in your bed tonight. You can have mine," I told him as I headed toward our bedroom. He didn't have to respond for me to know he'd heard me.

Evan surprised me the following day by seeing Tasmin again. On first meeting her, I would have figured the tanned, boyishly slender woman for more of a one-night conquest than a relationship prospect. Everything about her, to my eye, shouted "Rave Chick" and shouted it very plainly; the close-cropped indigo-colored hair, the frayed-hemmed hip huggers, the spiderwebs painted on her long, pointed fingernails, the platinum bicep bands and the garish inkings strategically tattooed over a fair third of her body. When it became apparent that Evan did not share my view, I grew to tolerate Tasmin's presence in our apartment.

I experimented with arranging to be elsewhere on days when I knew she'd be visiting, until avoiding her grew too tiresome. I said as little to Tasmin as I could on days when exposure to her was unavoidable, not so much because I disliked her, but because I feared her a little. Ludicrous though it may sound, despite my standing a full head taller than she, despite my outweighing her by at least forty pounds, she frightened me in the most inexpressible way. She seemed well aware of the disconcerting predatory quality in her eyes, and ultimately, pleased by it.

"Hey Aaron," she said to me one evening in our living room. I tend to sleep late on Saturdays, and had awoken unaware of her presence in the apartment.

"Hey," I replied, observing no reason to be rude. "Where's Evan?" I asked.

"Went to the city to bring back some wines," she replied, uncrossing exquisite legs on our sofa. For all my unrest in her company, Tasmin was supremely easy on the eyes. She gave the unoccupied cushion beside her a pat, inviting me to join her. For the first time, her eyes suggested nothing of the carnivore I'd taken her to be. The predator in her seemed caged for the moment. Still, I was unprepared to trust her fully. I offered her an excuse about wanting to take a shower, then turned to calmly flee without outwardly appearing to flee.

My ruse seemed to satisfy her momentarily.

Then she called my name, and I began to feel ill.

I regret having ignored my initial instinct to run without shame. It startled me to find Tasmin standing directly behind me, her body so close to mine that I scarcely avoided a collision as I turned. I hadn't heard her get off the sofa, which lie no less than fifteen feet from where I stood. Had I not been concentrating on the coolness of her hand as it cautiously ensnared my wrist, I might have appreciated the impossibility of her stealth and swiftness. Instead, I began trembling, still wrestling inwardly with precisely how she'd traveled nearly twenty feet in under a second without producing a sound.

Not a sound.

She smiled. "Before your shower, there's something you should see. Outside."

I offered her neither response nor resistance. I'd abandoned attempts to account for her baffling transit in favor of struggling to remember whether her lips had moved when she'd spoken a moment earlier. I didn't think they had, despite my having clearly heard every word she said.

Tasmin led me by the wrist through the living room, pausing once to select a large carrot from a fruit and vegetable bowl that Evan and I kept upon the kitchen table. Then she brought me out into the backyard where a crescent moon hung low in a deep lavender sky. The moist heat of the evening felt wonderful against the bareness of my chest and arms, but fell just short of conquering the chill that Tasmin's touch bred in me.

Observing nothing out of the ordinary in our yard apart from Tasmin herself, I asked her purpose in bringing me there. I was only now coming aware of the wrongness of my situation.

Pressing her lips tightly against my head, Tasmin whispered in my ear, sending an involuntary thrill along the entire left side of my body.

"I know you know," she said, confusing me.

Stepping away from me, she held up a fist, revealing to me a thumbnail terrifying in its jagged thickness. I watched her, my disbelief rooting me to the ground as she sank her thumbnail, which appeared to gain height by the second, deep into the flesh of her inner wrist. I'd moved beyond wondering at her ability to carry this out without any expression of pain. I felt as if a poorly chosen word would act upon my soul as a razor blade laid across my tongue would act upon the softness of my mouth.

Tasmin said, "I mean I'm aware that you fear me. I'm aware that you know there's something different about me. I've brought you here to show you very plainly where we stand, you and I."

The predator was loose. God help me, it was loose and firm-bodied and I could not outrun it even if I'd wanted to. However, the desire for escape was abandoning me, forsaking me against my will. Perhaps something in her voice and smile was robbing me of it.

Using her thumbnail, Tasmin opened her wrist. Her blood welled thick and black, overflowing the terrible chasm she was opening. The sight of her parting flesh was nothing compared to the loathsome sound that accompanied it; a torn, ragged hiss as the shiny painted nail carved soft meat. Under ordinary circumstances, I might have retched on the ground, but something prevented me from doing so.

I watched Tasmin splatter the soft carpet of grass with blood like ink. She did this with calculating intensity. Still no trace of pain furrowed her brow or pinched her lips, and that frightened me more than anything I'd seen.

My emotional dam burst at length and I yelled at her, demanded to know what in hell she was trying to do to herself. Ever unflappable, Tasmin smiled at me and said simply, "Wait. Watch."

So I did. I watched. We stood there and watched her blood pool for several moments, while she held my hand. Her skin still felt cold, despite the humidity of the night.

Her blood seeped into the grass and moist earth. I'd never felt so marooned as I did standing there with Tasmin.

"Wait? Wait for what? What are we supposed to be watching?" I demanded to know, "You need medical attention."

"No, you must wait and see all that I can be for Evan. . .and for you."

When next my gaze fell in search of her pooled blood, I found in its place a tiny, spreading patch of wildflowers. They clustered proudly, venturing outward to cover every inch of ground that had been touched by Tasmin's blood. If I observed them without blinking, I swore I could see the flowers growing taller straining upward as if in greeting, their indigo-colored petals unfolding as explosions of the plants continued to spring forth from the blood-soaked earth.

"I can be sweet, so sweet to you, to Evan. . .if given the chance," Tasmin told me. I said nothing, unable to think of any suitable response to the sight of her offering taking shape. Struck dumb, I could only watch the stems thicken, the leaves uncurl, born of her blood, nourished with her gaze.

"I can be kind until I'm forced to be otherwise," she told me, and brandished the carrot she'd lifted from the kitchen table. She placed its point against her navel, nestled it there firmly. Then she laid a finger against the opposite end of the carrot, and pressed the vegetable toward her body.

The almost total lightlessness did nothing to conceal what was transpiring before my eyes. I watched Tasmin slowly sink the carrot, watched her urge it gracefully into her. And as the thing vanished in increments, so did what remained of my sanity.

From somewhere deep inside Tasmin's body, I heard a sickening crunch as she pushed the carrot home, devouring it not through her mouth, but through her navel. I cursed my legs for refusing to carry me away, sparing me view of this woman's self-immolation. I resented her for having me witness such a grotesquery.

"You want it all, don't you?" she whispered once the entire carrot had been fed through her navel. I neither moved nor spoke. It was as much fear that kept me silent and immobile as it was my utter inability to command my muscles.

Only when Tasmin whispered "Go into your bedroom and undress, Aaron, and wait for me," did my legs remember how to walk, and once they were in motion, I could do no more to stop their progress than I could to stop my hands from removing my sweatpants and underwear. Searing pain attacked my heart as I saw Tasmin step into the unlit bedroom with me and lock the door behind her.

Her face had changed. Her eyes had dimmed and shrank into a reddened pair of sticky, clenching anal pores. A moist, smooth vulva had usurped the space ordinarily occupied by a woman's mouth and nose. Its folds pouted suggestively at me under the cold white stare of the moon.

"You'll have it all," She assured me in a phlegm-thick tone not entirely unpleasant.

And as she closed those puffy vertical lips on my mouth, clutched me by the shoulders, and ground the swollen clitoris against my nose, I finally grasped what was different about Tasmin.

She spent what seemed like hours tasting my most intimate physical locales, and did this utilizing at least three separate tongues, only one of which held residence in her mouth. I can elaborate no further without trembling. I will simply say that on that evening, Tasmin taught me more about the kinship and intimacies between rapture and agony than I would have thought possible. She taught me a great deal, cruel, succulent beast that she was, and I can remember several points throughout her lesson when despite my utter revulsion at my circumstance, I had to envy Evan.

My memory of my several couplings with Tasmin is not without its holes. One thing I do recall is that in all that time, be it all twenty minutes or all nine hours, my body was never mine to command. Only when Tasmin directed me to move or utter did I find myself capable of doing so. I couldn't even shed a self-pitying tear in the dark without permission. I'd been robbed of even that slightest of emotional releases by whatever strange sorcery was keeping my penis erect for my unwilling participation in Tasmin's game.

Once she'd grown bored with my subjugation, Tasmin knelt beside me and whispered into my ear. Her human lips glistened obscenely by moonlight spilling through the bedroom window.

"I promised I could be sweet, angel," she told me as mastery of my muscles was gradually relinquished to me. I struggled to turn my head, needing to see her. My voice had yet to resurface. "Evan hasn't experienced me half so thoroughly as you have," she said. Her tone of voice suggested I should feel honored by this admission. I could also tell that she was grinning at me in the dark. I wondered how many sets of teeth I might find in her mouth, were I able to turn fully and look.

Tasmin sat back in front of me on the bed, her legs folded underneath her, and regarded me with eyes of frigid jade. Moonlight pearlized the flawlessness of her skin and I fought to ignore the endless stream of blue images flooding my mind despite all I'd just been through.

"Rest now," Tasmin told me as she climbed off my bed and dressed. Immediately, I slipped into obedient slumber.

My first thought upon awakening was of the revolver boxed beneath my bed. I'd kept this single memento of my suicidal years a secret from Evan. In truth, I'd not thought about the gun in over a year. I'd never had reason to, until now.

Within seconds, I was out of bed with the loaded revolver, streaking nude toward the lewd sounds of lovemaking. Passing through the living room, I noted several emptied wine bottles upon the polished oak trunk table. A half-eaten cheesecake had been abandoned as well, along with a shattered wine flute and several articles of torn clothing. It seemed I'd slept for quite a while.

I found Tasmin and Evan naked together in the yard. The beauty of her rocking astride him defied description, and I warred with myself inwardly as I stepped onto the soft grass. Never had I seen a woman so feral, so ethereal as Tasmin. Never had I known such pain as she had visited upon me in that bedroom.

The night still burned as I crept toward them and lifted the revolver at the end of my arm, aligned it with Tasmin's face. Her eyes came open and through the tears filling my eyes, I watched her smile at me as I pulled the trigger. My bullet struck her just above her right eye, punching through her skull in two places as it departed through the rear of her head. Then more thick dark blood flowed, spraying out of the smoking holes I'd opened. Still glistening with sweat, Tasmin slumped to one side, struck the grass with her shoulder and lay still. That was when Evan began to shout and I began to make sounds akin to either laughter or crying. Maybe it was both at once.

"What have you done? What in God's name have you done?" he demanded of me.

I didn't bother to answer him. I knew there was no way I could tell him what had transpired in his absence. In his current state, he would never believe me, although I hoped that in time, I could sit with him and be believed when I told him my motives. I hoped he would realize some day that in committing this act for which I was sure to be jailed, I'd saved him from a lifetime of indignities of the sort to which I'd been subjected.

"Don't you know what she is?" I asked Evan later at the police precinct as a decidedly ornery officer fingerprinted me. I told Evan of her smile as I'd leveled the gun at her. I told him of her last words to me as I'd knelt over her cooling body to ensure that the damage inflicted by my bullet was not likely to be repaired.

"I don't die," she'd told me. Evan did not believe any of it. I supposed I could not blame him.

I haven't seen Evan since I was imprisoned. As I've said, tonight marks the one-year anniversary of the night I murdered Tasmin. I am told that the entire yard where Tasmin fell has been overtaken by indigo-colored wildflowers. I am told that there is not an inch of grass left uncovered by the blooms, which in time, grew up, over the house. So far, I hear no herbicide or chemical reagent has acted upon them with any effect. . .

Many a night has passed since then that I would not have been surprised to awaken and find her standing over my bed, the bullet holes in her shattered skull still smoldering. Many a night have I expected to open my eyes and watch that obscene rictus grin unzip across her face, or see her other face, the one composed of twin assholes and a vagina, descend toward mine and smother me to death with a kiss. There have been nights when I have hungered for her until my tears darkened my pillowcase, until my stomach cramped with my sobs. I believe she will return for me one night soon. I believe she will kneel upon my chest one night and inhale my soul as easily as a man sucks the smell of his favorite meal into his lungs.

Earlier tonight I found a flower sprouting between the stones in a dank, lightless corner of my cell. Its petals were the color of Tasmin's hair. The smile has not left my face since then, nor have I stopped crying. She will come for me, and I will resent her, I will fear her, I will beg her forgiveness when she returns. If I've learned one true thing from my dealings with Tasmin, it is that what this lady wants, she usually gets.

A subtle arch of one of her silver-studded eyebrows was Ashe's only indication that the lithe albino woman had heard his question. Whether he felt more intimidated by her silence or by her shaven head, or her multiple facial piercings and the solemn tightness of her jaw posed a riddle that Ashe had yet to solve. All he knew for certain was that the look on the woman's face asked very loudly if this fuckin' looked like the kind of fuckin' place that accepted fuckin' credit cards.

She stared through him a few seconds longer. Ashe felt himself flush, feeling further mortified by the second for having asked the question. Then, mercifully, the albino extended the leather-bound volume that she held, pulling it back the instant Ashe reached for it. His fingers closed embarrassingly on air.

"Payment up front," she barked, nailing him in place with arctic eyes. Ashe found the flat leather book neatly tucked under the albino's breadstick-thin arm, although he didn't remember seeing her place it there.

Digging into his sport coat pocket, Ashe withdrew a tightly rolled knot of twenty crisp one-hundred dollar bills, which he handed over to her, willing his hand steady. She handled the bundle for a moment, seeming to count it through sheer tactile contact, and that spooked Ashe as it always did. Indeed, if a single bill had been missing, Ashe had no doubt that she'd know instantly. She'd likely direct the establishment's two armed bouncers who wore their pistols in plain view to haul him back the way he'd come. Ashe couldn't figure out how in hell she did it, and didn't really care to know. He simply would not attempt to put one over on the albino.

Seeming as satisfied by the cash as by Ashe's timidity, the albino handed him the leather-bound catalogue. It felt lighter than usual. A slow night, it seemed.

"See me when you're ready," she said, her venomous eyes working their typical paralytic sorcery on Ashe. The slender woman turned, a cat changing direction in mid-leap, and strode away. The thick maple blocks of her boot heels clacked in a tight, measured cadence that seemed to overwhelm the acid-dripping metal music that played overhead and resounded through the cavernous catacombs of the place. Ashe opened the sacred leather-bound book, and his selection process began.

Not one eyebrow was ever lifted in suspicion over how it had happened that one night an empty lot sprawled, and the next, the black-painted building loomed in its place. No one really remembers when it went up, nor do they know whose authority erected it. As long as the place was jumping nightly, as long as it remained open until dawn, no one cared much about such trivialities.

"The Pulp Dungeon" seemed most befitting to name a nightclub whose interior had been decorated in meandering shades of red and magenta and black, and whose interior walls had, at no insignificant cost, been designed to ooze "blood" continuously. Membranous-looking organza festooned the place by the square mile. Slick-looking vinyl the color of kidneys and intestines wrapped everything from seat cushions to restroom doors, parodying exposed internal organs.

In the deepest shadows, the darkest corners of the place where the bloody red lighting failed to reach were where the lovers could be found. Predators grinning with bleached liar's teeth. Submissives sipping cups of vodka mixed with blood or semen, allowing strange fingers to explore their mouths, depositing vaginal juices, collared slaves lapping it from the fingertips of their mistresses. They could all be found here, drinking of each other, red light splashing them as they loved each other in pairs and groups, caring nothing for age or race or gender. All were welcome here that were in need of love, and here in the abysmal darkness, where blood and semen flowed like wine, all were one.

On the dance floor, faceless forms like lost souls swayed to music with too much bass in it. Here, a pair of women ground against each other, locked together by their dancing tongues. There, a lean, dark man whose body and shaven espresso-bean head glistened, rocked against a waifish redhead, his firm brown leg hugged tightly between her thighs as they thrashed. In the dark, new religions were blossoming. And in the basement, Ashe sat poring over photographs in a stylish leather-bound book.

Ashe had left himself two options. They were calling one "Luna." The other, they'd named "Val." Head and shoulders shots were Ashe's only aids in his selection process. Substandard lighting made it even more difficult to see, but Luna seemed like quite a delectable green-eyed scoop of ice cream. Buttermilk skin, bloodlessly pale, tight braids the color of amethyst, waifish frame. He reviewed her bio, finding everything he needed to know: Nineteen years old. Five feet nine. Pierced clit. Tattoos around her eyes and on their lids for the apparent purpose of perpetual shading. Ashe thought that unspeakably erotic for reasons difficult to articulate.

Val's appearance, however, could not be easily discounted. Six feet tall. Goatee. Hazel eyes. Latte-colored skin. Trim, hard shoulders into which Ashe imagined sinking his fingernails, slicing through firm red meat as he orgasmed into the dark youth. Val's appeal swelled, as did Ashe's erection.

Among this evening's rejects were "Stu," a ponytailed twenty-one-year-old Asian youth whose pallid skin seemed to barely resist splitting over the sharp blades and angles of his bones, and a chubby blonde of twenty-six years, whom they were calling "Nona." Besides being damned cute, Nona was listed as this collective's newest acquisition; less than an hour old. Likely to still be warm.

Ashe's gaze danced between the photos of Val and Luna for another second and then his choice was made. He summoned the albino, who'd spent the entire time draped upon a chaise lounge, observing him from across the room with an elitist's perfectly honed disinterest. Even after Ashe knew she'd noted his summoning gesture, the albino went on simply staring at him for another ten to fifteen seconds, before she moved to join him. Ashe ignored the unsubtle barb, and told her his selection.

"Please prepare Luna for this gentleman," the albino said, tossing the directive at the nearest of her henchman. A massive olive-skinned man, whose stiff, oily brush cut looked as if one could scour dirty casserole dishes with it, stalked away to do as he'd been told. The other bouncer, a dark man with jaundiced-looking eyes and a head that made Ashe think of milk chocolate Easter eggs, followed.

The albino led Ashe to a short corridor lined with unmarked doors on both walls. Eight doors in all; a tiny orange light bulb above each one. Pausing briefly before the room that Ashe would be occupying, she addressed him again, aloof demeanor never wavering, "As always, you will have forty minutes. One second longer than that, we reserve the right to interrupt and evict you. You'll find an unopened supply of petroleum jelly, baby oil, and water-based lubricants in the cabinets toward the rear of the room. Several types of condoms are available as well, although we don't recommend their usage with any oil-based products."

Ashe knew the speech well enough to recite it along with her, but didn't. He could fuck his selection of the evening bareback if he so desired, but under no circumstances was he to ejaculate inside Luna without a condom. The albino stressed that point twice, as if she were addressing an inattentive child. Then she was finished, and was striding away on those dopey heels of hers. Ashe twisted the doorknob and slipped inside.

A shiny drop of saliva, like a glass bead escaped Ashe's mouth, stretched elastically as he stepped into the small chilly room with its walls of bare cinderblock. Luna, his consort for the evening, awaited within upon a twin-sized rectangle of a cot. She was dressed in a black velvet minidress, a nice sleeveless number. Ashe would have gladly dropped another two grand to see her walk around in it. He regarded Luna, whose back lay pressed against the cool stone interior. Her head lolled to one side as if weighted by disinterest. Smeared shades of black and violet, like bruises, meandered across her tattooed eyelids. The tattoos made her skin seem all the paler by comparison, and Ashe could not restrain himself from touching them as he took a seat beside her.

“You’re lovely,” Ashe ventured, “Achingly lovely.” He stroked her eyelids with fingertips that barely trembled. Luna did not move. Luna did not speak. Ashe would never hear the voice that had partnered with such an attractive physical form. That knowledge was enough to ruin his experience here, though, so he closed his mind against it. Instead, he helped himself to a greedy, hungering eyeful of her calves, which looked toned enough to suggest she’d been into lightweight training, step classes, or some associated fitness regimen.

Kneeling as he was, Ashe might have been a pagan worshipper paying tribute to an ancient elemental deity. Luna certainly was fair enough to be a high priestess of old. But a gentle, lascivious bite on Luna’s knee would go in place of any pagan paeans tonight. His closed teeth on the coolness of her flesh failed to elicit a response from Luna, and this kind of passivity was but one of many issues that a different man might have considered drawbacks to engaging corpses in foreplay. But Ashe had his own tastes, and he felt no need to justify them to anyone too narrow-minded to understand.

Without shame, Ashe bent, again assuming his pagan worshipper’s crouch, and pressed his lips to the top of Luna’s foot, sucked gently and steadily, as if seeking to extract some form of nectar from her dead flesh. His tongue fluttered lightly over her skin. A living woman might have found the sensation arousing. There would be no giggling here, however. No playful, amorous wrestling or tumbling would ensue tonight, no expressions of affection, unless Ashe himself initiated them.

His lips crept toward Luna’s toes. Ashe pushed his tongue into the cold, tight crevices between each of them, relishing the feel, the taste of Luna’s dead foot in his mouth. His lips crept along her inner thighs, the smooth, hairless flesh thrilling Ashe as his fingertips roamed.

The skin at Luna’s throat felt thin, cold. Ashe closed his teeth on the curve of toned flesh where neck met shoulder. The neck was Ashe’s favorite part of the anatomy upon which to bestow love bites upon women and men alike. Unbidden images of a living Luna rose in Ashe's mind; her shivering with the pleasures of his lips and teeth, laughing as she twisted away from him and his tongue as he set it to work tickling the side of her neck, pressing her hot, wet mouth against his, engaging his renegade tongue with her own.

But none of this was to be. Luna was dead, and Ashe had been forever robbed of knowing her.

Ashe's thoughts returned inexorably to memories of his first lover, as they usually did whenever he found himself in a circumstance such as this one.

*****

Ashe entered life as the son of a fifteen-year-old single mother. As a child he never asked about his father. His mother used to allude to a tall, rugged rock guitarist with jet-black hair, and a smile like sunshine, but that story had always borne the undeniable stench of bullshit; even when Ashe was a child. Privately, he loathed the thought of sharing momma with a man, abhorred the thought of any male sleeping in her bed. Kissing her. Holding her hand. Ashe and Momma against the world was the way it had always been, and that was the way he had preferred it.

Ashe was barely twenty years old when she died, stolen from him by a brain aneurysm that cared nothing for Ashe's dependency on her smiles and laughter.

He'd spent several minutes standing over her in her bed that Saturday morning before realizing that her lungs were still. She was thirty-five years old, still shapely and firm-bodied. It still floored Ashe that such a young, vibrant creature had reared him, although familial pride comprised a mere portion of what he felt nowadays. His feelings toward Momma had not changed, but had certainly slanted. Puberty's onset had seen the advent of yet another emotion, a nameless presence inserted among the nobler, more traditional notions. Ashe may have lacked the maturity to effectively classify this aberration in himself, but there was no denying its hold on him.

Pressing his lips against the side of her face was the last thing he remembered, pressing his face into Momma's resilient breast, cursing himself for failing to will her back to life. Ashe told Momma that he loved her and that he was sorry he'd failed her.

Ashe had no idea, later on, how his tongue had found its way into her mouth. Neither did he recall what actions he'd taken after hiking her nightshirt up around her waist. Over the days and weeks and years to follow, he would forget his feelings of entitlement, as the only man in her life ever to really love her as she deserved. He would not remember ejaculating against her inner thigh. In time, his memories of her perfumed sweetness would fade. Ashe's only thought as he collapsed against the bared breasts of the luscious brunette who'd borne him, was that his first lover was dead. . .

*****

Ashe rocked back and forth against Luna's backside, having easily manipulated her slender frame into a kneeling position. Her head flopped against the mattress at a crazy angle as he pushed into her, her minidress pulled up over the pearlized paleness of her buttocks. Despite the petroleum jelly smearing his fingertips, Ashe's grasp on her narrow waist remained firm. His chest glistened with sweat. The piquant aroma of his own armpits stung his nostrils. Urgency filled him. His forty minutes were nearly concluded, and he did not wish to be interrupted.

When Ashe ejaculated, it was with tears scalding his eyes. His ragged cry sounded eerily like the word "Momma," as blended with an utterance more primal, almost feral. He held Luna against him while he spasmed, draining his scrotum into her. Even after so many visits to this place, Ashe still instinctively expected Luna to match his cries of release and pleasure and abandon with exclamations of her own.

Ashe grudgingly withdrew his sticky cock from her pinkness. He dressed quickly, tucked Luna's breasts back into the stretch minidress, adjusted the garment accordingly. Ashe knew that if he ever left one of the albino's prizes with a single hair out of place, he'd never again be allowed into the dungeon.

The albino woman's colorless eyes met his face like the smack of a closed fist as he passed her on his way upstairs to the main level of the Pulp club. He wondered if she somehow sensed that he'd worn no condom to contain his ejaculation. He hadn't deliberately disobeyed her. His mind had simply been elsewhere.

Ashe felt glad he'd come to the club tonight. This ritual always had such a cathartic effect on him. He thought of Momma, and wondered how she would feel about his lifestyle and what he'd become.

And what had he become? A man so terrified, so completely aghast at the notion of losing someone close to him that his affection should only be reserved for lovers who are already deceased? Was he merely the echo of an Oedipal young whelp with an appetite for forbidden intimacy, or something more? Ashe really didn't know anymore.

Sometimes dark things in Ashe tempted him to affirm such introspection. Sometimes his pleasures shamed him. There were nights when the empty eyes and utter unresponsiveness of his lovers would haunt his sleep, awaken him screaming, set him crying and vomiting. He still bore the scar of a wound he once inflicted on himself tumbling out of bed. That was the night he'd hallucinated that the eyeless wraith of a young boy called "Constantine," had sat up in bed beside him and spoken his name. Earlier that evening, Ashe had paid the albino woman two grand, and had sex with Constantine's corpse in the basement of the Pulp nightclub. The vision had evaporated at the sound of Ashe's scream, and Ashe needed to believe that the whole thing had been his imagination, so he'd devoted the days and weeks that followed to convincing himself of this. Part of him knew better, of course, but that part remained wisely mute most of the time, saying nothing of the fact that hallucinations do not typically leave the stench of putrefaction in their wake.

Upstairs, the darkness writhed. The clotted red light of the place made delicious obscenities of the sweat-slick arms and legs that tangled in the shadows. Soft sounds of suction kissed Ashe about the ears from the corners of rooms and clusters of overstuffed lounge furniture. Abandoned articles of clothing littered the dance floor, and a glistening groove had begun in that space where bare bodies shimmered red and angry and passionate. The sour-sweet scents of gin and everclear wafted from the wet pores and orifices of faceless legions, lending the air a permanent musk.

He watched the dance floor for another few seconds before leaving the club. As his eyes swept the hard, sticky bodies sprawling and twisting in the red light, Ashe wondered which of them he might soon spend time with in the basement. It seemed a night did not pass that someone didn't die within the club. They overdosed on drugs exotic and illegal. They committed suicide. Occasionally, people were murdered in the dark. Indeed, the frequent fatalities here were what the albino's basement enterprise was made of. Rarely were the bodies even missed. The general public cared nothing for what happened to junkies or drifters or runaways. Ashe cared, though. He cared enough to cradle their lifeless forms in his arms; enough to share acts of love with them from time to time; enough to weep for them afterward.

Ashe took a cleansing breath before beginning the long walk back to his home. The streets looked almost as desolate as he felt inside. He thought of Luna again, already beginning to miss her pale, cool skin, the taste of her dead flesh, the slick snugness of her rectum. As always, he immediately felt like a traitor to his mother, his first lover. No one, living or dead would ever mean to him as much as she had, or give to him as much as she'd given, even after she'd slipped beyond this life. Ashe wondered which spoke worse of him: that he was essentially cheating on a dead woman, or that he was cheating with other corpses rather than living partners capable of clutching him close and moaning and thrusting back at him when he loved them.

Overhead, a low crescent moon grinned knowingly at him, a sharpened scythe poised to fell the unfaithful. Ashe stuck to the shadows and did not look up at it again until he was safe at home.

When he slept, Ashe dreamed of a warm, living Luna, naked in his bed. He dreamed of touching her, feeling the heat and contraction of her pussy as he rocked against her. In the dream, his movements elicited her murmurs of satisfaction. It was more than any of the corpses in the albino's basement had ever expressed.

"Thank you for bringing me back," she whispered to him as they lay together in his dream, "The gift of life is the greatest that any person can give another. It's still in me."

Her tongue slipped into Ashe's mouth and shoved deep, warm and wet, and Ashe faded from consciousness, barely aware of the sharp cracking sound that accompanied a blossoming pain at the base of his skull as her foraging tongue punched through it.

The sun rose early the next morning. The weather forecasts called for another clear, humid day.

All over town, people awoke, climbed from their beds feeling great or feeling lousy. People showered or they didn't, got dressed and went off to another day of work or personal errands. Many picked up a cup of coffee and a newspaper on their way. More than half of those who did, were shocked at the headline reading "LOCAL PRIEST DISCOVERED DEAD IN HOME." All over town, people holding newspapers hurriedly turned to the page where the article was listed. There, they found the details of how Father Ashe Worthing, thirty-nine years old, ordained priest and principal of the Holy College of the Ascension had been found in his bed, dead of causes currently unknown. The article referred to the circumstances surrounding the Father's demise as "under investigation," stating that although the possibility could not be ruled out, the case did not appear at this time, to have been a homicide. . .

*****

Evening fell on the city like a damp, dark blanket. Outside the unmarked entrance to the club called "The Pulp Dungeon," moonlight glazed glossy bodies draped in melancholy silks and lace. The Goth girl seated behind the first cashier window was turned sideways, giggling wildly at something the slender male cashier beside her was saying. When she looked up, a patron was standing patiently in front of her window holding a twenty-dollar bill, and the Goth cleared her throat before offering a curt apology.

"How many?" the cashier asked, and waited to be told how many admittances the slim waifish girl with the amethyst colored braids was purchasing. She had cool tattoos around the eyes, the Goth thought.

"One," Luna told her.

THROUGH THE EYES OF SEPTEMBER

"They say that if you look long enough at it, she'll smile for you."

Black nothingness loomed beyond the woman in the gallery photograph. With shadows protecting her modesty like jealous lovers, the model pouted in nude black-and-white splendor. The bottom border of the twenty-four-by-thirty-two photograph bore the name of the artist who'd titled the artwork "September."

She reposed in a seductive sprawl that offered art lovers the most breathtaking view of her derrière, her face cast backward over her left shoulder as if in afterthought. Her dark eyes stared beyond the edge of the photo, fixed on something or someone she appeared to regard as prey.

Jude's voice had joined his chubby, ponytailed gullibility in grating on Damian's nerves. "Who said it? Who are 'they'?" Damian demanded.

Granules of the sand in which she knelt encrusted the backs of her thighs, the sensuous delicacy of her ass. Glinting in the downward-cast light employed by her photographer, the sand made a confection of her flesh, as if she'd rolled herself in sugar.

Ignoring the questions, Jude pulled a handful of Reese's pieces from the pocket of his army drab duster and continued, munching noisily. "Gotta keep your thoughts pure and on her alone, though, or she'll lay a curse on you with those eyes of hers. God, she's gorgeous."

"Whoever 'they' are, I think 'they' are full of shit. Who the hell believes in curses anymore, anyway?" Damian fumed. If there existed one animal he truly despised, it was an unemployed Jude. Today marked three weeks since the stupid bastard let his fucking numerologist convince him that his delivery job motorcycling floral arrangements around Manhattan was playing hell with his "life path." Gullible fuck resigned that same day.

The model's pose and facial fixture demanded tribute. Something regal in the artful flow of her lines and hues challenged the senses not only to appreciate her, but to wonder about her. Was it lust sweat or April rain that lent her body its glow? Was "September" her name, or did the word hold other significance? What did her sex smell like after she fucked hard? Has she a patient, ravenous lover to whom her most intimate secrets are entrusted?

Damian found himself wondering about her as Jude prattled on.

"I'm just telling you what they say, that's all. They also say that the photographer went mad shortly after taking the picture; trashed his gear, destroyed all his negatives, burned himself to death torching his studio. That's why the picture's priced so damn high. It was the only thing to survive the fire. Believe or don't believe. But don't say I didn't warn you." Jude weighted his tone with mock foreboding. Damian could have done without the ribbing, and fired a bullet-lethal glance at Jude, communicating as much.

Given a second opportunity to consider having Jude accompany him to this erotic art exhibit, Damian would have gone alone. It affected his mood little to know he probably needed the company as much as Jude did. Damian wasn't the only one walking wounded these days, but he was sure as hell the only one he could muster any sympathy for. Charisse had been right to leave a selfish bastard like him. The absence of her cocoa-skinned breathlessness astride him at night still chewed upon Damian's heart. It still throbbed like an insect bite upon the mind, further chafed by his every remembrance of lazy Sunday mornings spent inside her. He couldn't deny her being better off for their breakup, though, and that hurt worse than anything.

Jude sidled closer to Damian, sensing his friend's darkening mood the way a rabbit senses bad weather in the wind. "So be honest," he leered, "Think Miss 'September' was ever into threesomes?"

“Do I think she ‘*was*’ into them? What is she, dead?” Damian regretted the snipe even as it escaped his lips. Too much vitality lived in her skin for the woman in the photo to be dead.

“That’s what they say. They say she was a witch who murdered her unfaithful lover who was also a witch, and then committed suicide.”

“Damn shame,” a heartbroken Damian sighed, “if it’s true.” He wondered whether she was really dead, really a witch. If one stared at her, he supposed her eyes did embody something of the infectious sensuality one would expect in a sorceress.

Less devastated, apparently, than Damian felt, Jude quickly asked, “Witches, they’re into threesomes and orgies, right? I mean like, as part of their rituals and shit?”

“How would I know?” Damian shrugged. Suddenly, he could bear the sight of the model in the photo no longer. Whether or not Jude was full of shit didn’t matter. Departed was Damian’s ability to view her without feeling mournful. It was the way he would imagine feeling in the company of a lover suffering with terminal illness.

“She’s fuckin’ gorgeous, isn’t she?” Jude smiled crookedly as they moved to the next exhibit.

“She *was*, yes.” Damian replied.

“Looks familiar, too,” Jude added, “Got a sweet little rack.”

“What?” Damian tore himself from “September” to find Jude admiring not the photo, but a lone brunette standing across the gallery beside the erotica sculpture exhibit. Her petite frame left the girl looking young enough to be a minor, although her dress of black low-cut lace and the filled champagne flute she held suggested otherwise.

Before he could comment on Jude’s assessment of the “rack” in question, Damian found his eyes had returned to the photo. A jarring taste mimicking ashes and wet pussy smoldered low in his throat like phantom maggots crowding his esophagus. Menstrual sourness besieged his tongue. The foul taste climbed like poison toward his brain as he found himself stealing a few more seconds with "September." Damian doubled into silent dry-retching. He couldn't take his eyes off the witch.

Several feet away, Damian overheard Jude, having joined the familiar-looking brunette, exclaim "They say that by the time Picasso died, he had created twenty-two thousand works of art. . ."

*****

"September" stared into nothingness, her features all but obscured by the darkness of Damian's bedroom. The black velvet drapes above his windows conspired with the approaching night to pack the room with shadows. The model's expression told a different story now than it had at the gallery one week ago. Tonight, her flat black eyes whispered tales of a feral she-beast no less dangerous for being on her knees. Tonight, the flexed firmness of her buttocks and calves menaced as if at any moment she might spring from her photograph in pursuit of experiences best hunted in darkness.

The cedar-mounted photo had cost him eight hundred seventy dollars. Jude still thought him crazy for having purchased her, still joked that while a dead and naked witch surely marked notable improvement in Damian's taste in girlfriends, a man should never have to buy a woman's companionship. Jude's humor remained one of his many traits to which Damian bore certain time-tempered immunity. The shine of her thighs and luxuriant slopes of her shoulders and back spoke louder than feeble humor.

Her benefactor approached the easel upon which he maintained her. She was his now to admire. Though gawkers like Jude would never appreciate any quality beyond her nakedness, Damian recognized depths unspoken in the fixture of her face, the passive dominance in her positioning.

Dustings every two hours, coupled with Damian's nightly once-over using damp terrycloth worked well toward keeping "September" dust-free. Damian knelt before the easel, paying tribute at his altar. At her shrine. Bowing his head, he gripped the cedar-mounted photograph at its edges, pulled it against his chest as he rose to his feet, his mindless murmurs swimming through the blackness like mutant eels through murky water.

"Maybe tonight, love? Will you smile for me tonight?" Damian begged the photograph in his arms, "Please, love, let it be tonight."

The eyes of "September" remained fixed on something just beyond her view and his. Her pout betrayed arrogance tonight, as if Damian and his affections fell so far beneath her concern that she felt him unworthy even of eye contact. Her ass seemed to taunt, its rising curvature offered, yet not fully surrendered, by the loving shadows that clung to the woman's skin. Damian's heart felt like a stone sinking into his gut.

His telephone sounded, cleaving his melancholy. Resentful of the intrusion on his personal time with "September," he made no move to answer it. It was probably Jude calling with more conspiracy theories about extraterrestrials infiltrating Hollywood. Jude could be such a stupid bastard. Two rings later, the phone's answering machine clacked into action.

Through white noise fraying the caller's words, he made out "Damian, it's Randi. If you're there, pick up the phone."

Randi? Randi who? Damian wrestled with the question until the caller spoke again. The voice sounded helium-afflicted; the lyricism of an adolescent girl's tone joined with the assertive sophistication of a woman's. Given the breathless bounce of her words, she was outdoors, calling from a mobile phone and striding at a good clip.

"I'm on my way to your place. Just got out of work," Randi huffed, "Got stuck with overtime." Portions of her explanation drowned in the background blaring of automobile horns. Damian heard bus engines grumble idly, sounding annoyed by the swelling whine of a passing ambulance's siren. Randi was crossing a street. He still couldn't recall who she was. These days, "September's" legs stayed wrapped too tightly around his mind for Damian to recall much of anything apart from her. There were nights when remembering his own name was tedium enough.

Then he remembered the perfume she'd worn to the erotica exhibit, and that sensation of stones sinking in his gut resurfaced, revisiting its imagined weight upon his vital organs.

The familiar-looking brunette with the fluffy tied-back hair and "Fuck-me-standing" hips worked at the coffee bar he sometimes visited on Saint Mark's Place at Third Avenue. On the night he and Jude bumped into her at the art exhibit, they learned her name. Jude wasted little time or subtlety on letting Randi know that Damian was available.

They'd had one date; spent most of it drunk and fucking in the bed of a friend she apartment-sat for last month. He'd only pursued her so Jude would quit riding him about how exploring new relationships would help him get over Charisse. Easy for *him* to say.

The walk to his apartment would take her less than fifteen minutes. Damian dove for the telephone before she could end the call. Tonight was to be their second date and damn if it hadn't slipped his mind.

"Randi?"

"Damian!" she bubbled.

"Hey," he stammered, still simmering privately over "September's" ongoing refusal to smile for him. What wonders would he find, looking through the witch's eyes, seeing whatever captivated her from beyond the photo's edge? He needed to know. . .

Randi told him "I'm glad we're meeting tonight."

"Rough workday today?"

"Let's just say I could use a bit of relaxation." She allowed the ghost of a pause before the last word; delivered it in a slanting tone that belied dual implications. Her message was clear: she had stresses she needed to fuck away, and Damian was accessible. Tonight, he had some as well, although how many beers he'd have to finish before he could bed her without feeling unfaithful to "September" was anyone's guess.

Damian told her, "I'll be waiting," and hung up the phone, wanting sex. He gave "September" a final wipe and removed it from the easel. He brought it to his bedroom closet, where he entombed the witch's photo in that lightless recess. The witch's beauty belonged to him, even if she *never* deigned to smile for him or meet his eye. He would burn the damned photo before he'd share her with another. Not even to Jude had Damian allowed the briefest glimpse of "September" since purchasing the photo. Randi would enjoy no such privilege either.

"Forgive me," he told the witch before sealing "September" inside, "for things I might do tonight, not out of desire, but out of need." Damian closed and locked the closet door.

Had the first tears of guilt not flooded his eyes just then, Damian would have met the witch's unblinking stare as it sought to burn accusing holes into his skull.

*****

Garish neon beer advertisements packed into the establishment's front window spilled light onto the vomit-sour Bowery sidewalk. Rainwater puddles collected luminous logos for Budweiser, Corona, and various Lagers. The bourbon-laced chicken wings served within, flavored in a patron's choice of either "Wimpmeat" or "Ass-kickin'" barbecue sauce, remained a staple at the bar called Original's Inn. The sweet potato skins loaded with cheddar and chives were poetry by bar food standards, although the beer-batter-fried Charleston Chew never failed to win visitors over, as it remained the only dessert on the establishment's menu. The food compensated with spice for what it lacked in presentation, just as Original's Inn compensated for its food with fifty-cent well drinks and live entertainment on Friday nights.

The acid jazz quartet onstage in the darkened basement lounge flooded the space with evocative grooves. It wasn't the Goth metal band that Randi had talked about seeing next time the group toured New York City, but she seemed to be digging the show as much as Damian was digging her hand in his lap.

"A toast," she told him, lifting her third Vodka Martini, "To Dionysus, god of wine and ecstasy, son of the Moon."

“Cheers,” Damian replied, clinking his second pint of Guinness against her glass.

“We’re supposed to capture the moon’s reflection in our cups,” Randi smiled.

“What do we do with it once we’ve caught it?”

“We raise it up in salutation, then drink in her essence.”

“Her?”

“The moon’s. Then we close our eyes and feel the presence of the God and Goddess coursing through us.”

Two pints of Guinness and two Long Island Iced Teas had Damian wanting to catch the moon’s essence indeed, but in Randi’s eyes rather than a glass of beer.

“I’m sold, although before we catch any moonbeams, we better think about catching some sky. Moonbeams hardly ever come in here anymore; not since the owners took the condom machines out of the bathrooms.” Randi’s mouth laughed at the joke. Her eyes licked his neck.

“Let’s lose this place, then. We’ll go bathe in moonlight,” Randi prompted, already scooting out of her seat. Original’s Inn wasn’t without its charm, but tonight, she felt it was best appreciated fading in the rear view mirror of a taxi. Damian took little convincing.

*****

The taxi’s interior stank of fried-foods and the oily paper bags in which they’d been served. When the driver asked their destination, Damian waited to hear Randi’s answer.

“Your place,” she whispered to him. He told the driver his address. The man glanced at the inebriated lady before leveling a gaze at Damian that had “You lucky asshole” written all over it.

“What’s so funny?” Randi asked, hearing Damian chuckle at the driver’s unspoken sentiment. It was the first laugh he’d had in days that hadn’t felt forced.

“Nothing.”

*****

Before long, darkness claimed them. Fingers shoved. Flesh yielded to careless teeth. Dionysus winked along the moist pinkness of avaricious tongues.

Like writhing infants in night’s womb, Randi and Damian braided limbs beneath black sheets. Nestled in competitive fuck, they razed one another’s boundaries without shame or apology.

Arousal musk spiced their palates. Abandoned grunts perfumed Damian’s bedroom. Their liquor-laced epithets thickened the air. Sucking sweat from leather-cinched wrists, they composed odes to clenched hips and straining lungs.

Licking bite marks that perforated shoulders and inner thighs, they were origami dancers. They were salacious acrobats performing chest to back in the spotlight, ass to belly on a creaking king-sized stage.

And the eyes of “September” wafted into his head, their phantom as lithe and surreptitious as the burning smell stealing through the partly-open window. In the dirt lot across the street, transients often pitched bonfires in rubbish drums for warmth. They did this when it was cold, though; not on Indian summer nights like this one.

Those unsmiling eyes burrowing about in his brain unsettled him the way smelling a former lover’s perfume on someone new discomfits the nostrils. He fought to ignore the accusing glare. He fought to concentrate on the delicious hottie mashing her sweaty tits against his mouth. Damian coughed against Randi’s stomach an instant before she too, began choking on smoke.

“Damian, my God! Your closet!. . .”

Damian bolted to his feet. An acrid burning stench ripped his sinuses. The burning smell wasn't wafting in from outside. It was Damian's bedroom that was on fire.

Rising plumes of black cumulus uncurled from underneath the closet door, clotting the atmosphere. Faint crackling foreboded from within the closet's confines. He thought of the witch in the photograph. Would she survive a second fire?

Had she *started* the fire?

"Get out," he told Randi, ushering her out of bed, "Into the other room. You'll be safe there. I can handle this."

Snatching up all her clothing, wriggling into every other article, Randi said, "Are you *kidding*? You need the fire department!"

"I'll be all right." He wasn't leaving. Not without "September."

Damian tore open the closet door, ripping the knob free in his haste. Its burning metal skin seared his palm with a belligerent hiss. He swore, hurling it into darkness. Flames leapt and flared, gorging on oxygen that gusted through the opened door in an asthmatic huff. The fire was an entity, contentedly feeding on Damian's clothing and acquisitions as if possessing perfect right to them. It spewed vitriolic black smoke up his nostrils as if defending itself from an attacker. Resting unharmed amidst the licking orange tongues of fire, "September" glared up at him, feral as ever.

So you do *care*, he gloated silently, vindication like an electrical current coursing through him. For all the witch's offish posturing, it seemed that even the departed were capable of jealousy. Leaning into the inferno, Damian drew his lungs full of smoke, relishing its fetor like perfume, savoring "September's" apparent discontentment like the scent of roses.

The swelling flames beckoned to him. The seductive undulation of orange tongues seemed to invite him in; in where the warmth was, in where it was always September, where love never died. Damian risked a step forward, scarcely aware of the agitation slanting Randi's voice as she rushed back from his kitchen. She spoke again.

"I said, *move it!* I'm trying to help you here."

Damian got jostled aside an instant before Randi dumped a pitcherful of bathroom tap water into the closet to drown the twisting sirens at play in there. "September" took most of the salvo, and what water didn't run down her cedar-mounted back and ass to quench the smoldering hit its targets dead-on.

Once, the fire was dead, Randi asked "Damian, are you all right? Didn't you hear me telling you to back off before you got burned?"

"Guess I panicked," he lied. Those flames were still burning inside his head, painting ardent hipswirls of lovelight along the inner walls of his skull.

"Well at least neither of us burned. What do you think start—"

"I'd like you to leave now." Damian quietly told her, knowing how harsh it sounded but unable to care. She'd thrown water in "September's" face? What the fuck was she thinking?

"What? Just like that? You want me to leave?"

"Now, yes." Guilt weighted his gaze, made it too heavy to lift, and so he studied his toes as he spoke. Keeping his eyes averted protected Damian from the hurt he knew her eyes held, but offered no defense against that in Randi's voice. They'd begun to care for each other a little and here he was fucking it up.

"Sure. Screw me cross-eyed, then kick me the fuck out right after I save your life, right? You heartless asshole."

"No argument here. Good night."

*****

The first thing he did, finding himself alone again, was strip the sheets from his bed. These found a quick home outside on the fire escape, rather than in the musty corner of the room to which soiled linens got routinely banished. Perhaps the gathering night winds would carry the stink of sweat and pussy away from the sheets, perhaps not. Either way, Damian could no longer bear their sight or damp odor.

He retrieved "September" from the sodden garment pile in his closet. Her eyes held his as if gauging his handling, as if his slightest misstep would cost him every future happiness. How dare that bitch throw water in her face!

Resting upon the sill of the open window, Damian drew his knees up and cradled the portrait in his lap, tracing the witch's curvature and slope with his fingers. With his eyes closed, the laminate was warm skin, seductively tensile, shuddering under his caress. He felt her muscles shift beneath taut skin, could smell moist female flesh on his fingertips when he touched his nose. . .

Realization jolted him to his feet. *He'd felt skin! He'd touched real skin! However impossibly, by whatever unknowable sorcery, his hands had sampled her flesh!!*

Damian's eyes snapped open as he snatched away his hand, swearing in stark, lusting terror. "September" clattered to the floor. When he retrieved it, the photo's gaze no longer favored him as it had when his closet was burning. "September's" gaze had returned to whatever curiosity lie beyond the portrait's edge.

"But. . ." Damian began, shaking with dismay, "No. . .please. You looked at me. You *did.* I *saw* your eyes looking at me."

The witch mocked him with her muteness. Even naked on her knees, she commanded more authority than Damian ever had or would. He resented her for that. He worshipped her because of that.

"Look at me again. . .please?" he begged, "Please, *please* look again! Don't have to smile. Just. . .let me know you're in there?"

Damian reeled and doubled on legs that suddenly held all the supportive strength of two columns of flan. His stomach grew hot as he sank to his knees. A calculated kind of wretchedness assaulted him; a stomachful of twisting briars, his pulse deafening like arrythmic tribal drums, napalm sweat springing forth to scald his pores. Was this his punishment for mishandling “September” moments ago?

His bedroom rippled in and out of focus like a scrying pool revelation. Damian clenched his teeth together as if they might dam the rushing plume of vomit streaking up his esophagus. They didn’t, and Damian retched and shook as his dinner erupted into the moonlight. Its vile paste splattered his hands, webbed his fingers, stinking horribly of putrid liquor and bile. Its vapors stung his nostrils, rallied shaming tears to spill down his cheeks.

The nude woman’s gray laminate eyes maintained their rapt study of the unknowable as Damian lay watching his regurgitations pool with froth-flecked lips. The sand encrusting her ass looked so damned much like sugar. What would he give for a taste? How many lovers has she anointed with the perspiration responsible for her body’s shine?

Then. . .movement from the pool of vomit. Damian watched them with skeptical eyes. Maggots. Writhing through the curdled broth. Scores of them. Hundreds. Mucus-slick, creeping blind through the undigested remains of Damian’s venison quesadilla.

Damian blinked away tears, too sickened to move, and retched again so hard that he couldn’t breathe. The maggots piled clumsily onto one another as they burrowed about through the purulent sludge. Their operations bore the distinction of vigorously rehearsed maneuvers as they loped into a loose interpretation of the letter “U.” This formation, they seemed to hold until satisfied that their point had been taken, before dispersing to mill about for a bit before reorganizing themselves into a frenetic “R.”

“N” came next, followed in due course by the letters “O” and lowercase “t.” Damian didn’t dare pull his eyes away from them until their message was completed. Had his legs cooperated with his brain, he might have run. But something wasn’t letting him, was forcing him to bear witness as the slimy maggots assembled and reassembled in their maniac’s parody of football cheerleaders at halftime. By the time the blind parasites reached the final letter, his fear had ebbed almost completely, supplanted by the most heartfelt sense of mortification he’d ever felt.

'*U R Not WorTHy*,' the vomit-caked maggots accused him.

Shamed by this latest repudiation, Damian left the room on his knees. He had to piss, but more importantly, he needed to release the tears brimming in his eyes, but damn if he'd be caught dead crying in front of the witch. Her parasites were wrong about him.

The bathroom electricity whined and coughed as if Damian's flip of the light switch had caught it in a moment of frenzied indecision. Damian scarcely had time to shield his eyes before the smudged light bulb fixed above the mirror exploded into a million radiant shards that dusted the floor, wash, basin and adjacent toilet commode. He'd have to remember to remove and replace the broken bulb in the morning. At present, fluorescent lighting was non-essential. He'd been peeing in the dark in this bathroom for years.

Damian lifted the toilet lid, aimed, and flowed. When finished, he washed his hands and left without flushing.

The message was wrong. He *was* worthy, damn it! Tonight, "September's" eyes had touched him. Their love was ephemeral, but affection was affection, and the simple fact that she'd finally looked his way, if even for the space of a heartbeat, was good enough for Damian, if not for storybook romance standards.

Damian placed her photo upon the bed, carefully positioning it over the hole in his mattress. He climbed over her on his knees and uncapped a plastic vial he kept at bedside. His erection bulged painfully as he aligned the felt-rimmed orifice he'd carved in the triangle of shadow between her buttocks with the hole he'd bored in his mattress.

She'd loved him enough to turn her eyes upon him earlier tonight. The time had arrived for him to illustrate the measure of his worthiness.

Damian tipped the bottle, dribbled a viscous stream of unscented lube into the mattress' fuckhole. "September" looked relaxed and ready as he massaged oil into his rigid manhood. She seemed disinterested, undisturbed by the implication, but

Damian knew differently. Why would she have manifested herself to him if she didn't want this as much as he?

The witch wanted his cock. She *had* to. She wanted his ejaculation pumped into her, his fervor burning her skin, but Damian recognized her position as one of Earth's new goddesses, and realized that such stature precluded her from deigning to such admissions. No matter. If ever a relationship was joined that demanded consummation, then surely theirs did. Tonight. Right here. Right now. She didn't have to react to him. Damian could *sense* her anticipation like a pheromone. . .

Damian guided his swollen cock downward, pushing through cedar, sinking through the felt-lined ring of the orifice he'd carved. Studiously, he pressed his erection through his cedar-mounted photograph of seduction made flesh, and down into the oil-soaked mattress padding serving him as her vagina.

U R Not WorTHy, whined the doomsayer at his core.

Damian's hips descended cautiously. His length plumbed "September's" depth, as he loomed above her, listening, watching her eyes for reaction. His rhythms unfurled with an affectionate fluidity markedly missing from his undressed audiences with Randi.

Conveniently accessible boozehounds who take it up the ass on the first date weren't without their merits, but the kind of uncomplicated screw he enjoyed with Randi would never compare with sleeping inside an immortal sorceress. Gliding deep into "September," Damian knew he'd chosen wisely.

Unworthy indeed, he grinned into "September's" hair as he orgasmed and lost consciousness.

*****

"Oh my God. It's him. It's Damian," was all the young woman who'd called them to the apartment could manage before collapsing into tears. Yawning before them, the bedroom was a prison of foul air and juicy buzzing flies. The flesh-draped skeleton shivering naked upon the bed barely acknowledged the emergency medical techs who rushed past Randi to check its vitals. It had no idea that its name had once been Damian, or that it had once had friends, family, a job, an apartment; that it had once been a man.

Damian's telephone lay shattered in a piss-sticky corner of the bedroom where he'd flung it eight nights ago. He'd lost patience with the damn thing ringing while he and "September" were making love. The concerned voices that whined through the messages it recorded held no importance. He knew no "Jude," no "Mom," no "Charisse," nor did this new anti-Damian need any. Anti-Damian couldn't care less about having been fired from his job for absence, or being forgiven by the one called "Charisse," or about her apparently renewed hope that they might "try again," whatever the fuck that meant.

His last moments as Damian had seen him lose patience with many things, not the least of which was personal grooming. Amenities such as washing and toilets held less importance than remaining within constant company of "September," and the thing of slack skin and tremulous bones eyed the EMT's warily as they pressed sterile gauze against his bloodied regions.

Randi scrambled onto his bed, kissed Damian's brow, cooed to him in reassuring tones. She made a good show of it, even if the mere sight of him did tempt her to vomit. Look what the fuck he'd done to the painting! Her painting! Meanwhile, the EMTs instructed one another in solemn tones as Damian was transferred to a stretcher and secured into place. They probably saw this sort of thing all the time.

The odors of shit and urine sang throughout the apartment. Their atmosphere carried a dead smell also, that spoke to the hearts of all in attendance whenever anyone looked Damian's way; while the poor bastard continued to draw breath, his present condition fell a damn sight short of his being alive. Thick smears of dried feces clung to his asscheeks, caked the blood-and-piss-sodden mattress Damian shared with a large cedar-mounted photograph of a nude model. A pool of dried vomit cracked beneath the feet of the uniformed rescuers tending to him. Behind the vacant windows of Damian's eyes, a lost child sought to comprehend the sudden cacophony of faces and loud, rude sounds assaulting him.

None who noticed the hole in the picture spoke of it. Not after glimpsing the soiled hole gouged in his threadbare mattress, the fresh blood caking his penis. No, the withered husk being strapped down before them all; this was not a man alive. This was not a man at all.

"Have you fallen?" Damian mouthed at the EMTs, finding his tongue and throat too dry to lend voice to the question.

"Will you be riding in the ambulance with him, miss?" Randi was asked.

"No. I'll meet you at the hospital." she lied.

"All right, then. We'll be moving him in just a moment," the senior Technician told her on his way out of the room.

"Have you fallen through the eyes of 'September'?" Damian asked Randi without seeing her or realizing they were alone for a moment.

"Indra," she whispered to him, "In those days," she nodded toward the photo, "My name was Indra. The charmer."

Damian gaped at Randi with unseeing eyes. In another time, in another life, he might have appreciated the similarities between the two names.

She knelt beside the gurney, positioning herself to better pour her hemlock whispers into his ear. "I went to the art exhibit that night seeking to buy the photo you've desecrated. I've outlived more corporeal vessels than you'd imagine, but that one; the one in that photograph was my favorite by far. Did you know she was once engaged to an Italian Duke? And still, I was prepared to outlive this little twat's body as your lover and equal."

"I'd like you to leave now," she whispered into his ear.

Rearranging her facial fixture to that of the concerned girlfriend that had greeted the emergency medical workers, Randi watched Damian until he stopped breathing, her obedient worshipper proving his worth and devotion for all time.

RELIQUARY

He knew it was bad when Thora, who lived a thirty-minute seventy miles-per-hour drive outside of town, arrived at his place a scant eight minutes after phoning him. The knuckles rapping out “shave and a haircut” against his apartment door despite the presence of a perfectly functional and melodious doorbell could belong to no one else.

Alton, tired as always of being a patsy, opened the door, unable as always to do otherwise. Such was the natural order of his relationship with Thora; her sailor’s sense of humor and trophy wife physical characteristics, occasions to which Alton always rose lusting. To believe, though, that the term “relationship” could be applied to him and Thora in anything other than the loosest and most generous of regards, he’d have been twice the fool. Luckily for him, no such delusion had ever distorted his view.

“I hope you’re still a Jim Beam man,” she said, bounding across his threshold before he could greet her.

“It’s that bad, is it?” he asked the air as she made for the bottles of liquor that she knew he kept in his kitchen.

“First, a drink. Then we’ll talk,” she decreed, selecting two glasses from his cabinet. “You in or out?” she demanded, lifting one toward Alton, filling the other for herself.

“I’m in. On the rocks.”

“Pansy.”

Thora raided his freezer, handed Alton his glass of fire and ice.

"So here's the thing," she said, wading into a recounting of her husband Horace's latest marital misstep. Less because he cared than because this prelude to her real purpose in coming here had always gone in place of physical foreplay, Alton pretended to listen. He pretended to empathize, and did so in a manner deserving of Academy Award recognition. It was what he'd always done, just as coming here to revenge herself against a husband who, as she explained it, just didn't "get" her, was what Thora had always done.

As for what parent would, upon first glimpse of a newborn baby boy, choose to name the kid "Horace," it seemed such an unmitigated cruelty that Alton hadn't stopped laughing since the day of his and Thora's introduction. Horace, it seemed, had been blessed with pockets of more than sufficient depth to keep Thora dripping with rare gems and haute couture. He liked, as she frequently put it, "to keep his trophy polished." The truth, or the version of it that Thora had convinced herself was fact, was that he might have exchanged wedding vows with her more than a decade ago on the shores of some South Pacific island or the other, but he had never married Thora. At best, she was and would always be his mistress. The software company he'd founded longer ago than Alton had been alive would always be Horace's first love and only recognized spouse.

It was an indignity that Thora took out on Alton at every opportunity, and one for which he could not, despite his best efforts, pity her, given the rewards that it afforded him.

*****

Sovereignty was hers in his bed. Between his bedsheets lie her empire of unsheathed claws and naked edicts to be disobeyed only at a gambling man's peril; an escapist autocracy designed for the sole purpose of punctuating to an interested lover her relevance and potency. Her throne was his jutting erection, that testament to her royal stature from which she passed down the laws of the land. Bouncing astride him, her waist gripped with as much fever as a beggar's alms, she was *someone's* queen, if not Horace's. With Alton's arms about her, him battering her from behind and fucking her ears with covetous filth that struck as deeply at her core as his pelvic stabs, Thora mattered in a way she scarcely did in her own bed. To matter was as much as she could hope for. To join her in the pretense that she did was as much of himself as Alton dared to devote to their shared folly. In a relationship that was by no stretch of the imagination a "relationship," to give or be more to her than a convenient cock to ascend whenever the fancy took her, was death. In adult film industry vernacular, he was a "stunt dick," a substitute hardness that got called into play upon failure of his woman's intended partner to perform. To surrender to any greater emotional investment in screwing another man's wife than to pull her hair when her clutch raised welts across his shoulders, was lunacy. Alton felt too young to die or yet go insane.

Handcuffed to his bedposts, Alton was her obedient manservant, the star upon which her bronze hips and sable hair swung, his thickness her treasure buried in places that made her come at volumes that surely lacked a noblewoman's dignity. When his tongue and fingertips pushed into her ass, snowbound foragers seeking warmth for survival, Alton was her knight, her rogue realm defender tipping his lance against her tyranny, his plots overthrowing her by the inch, leaving Thora's nipples taut, her thighs sticky and quaking with rage and abdication. Nights that loaded his kisses with vodka and wine appointed him alchemist of her court, bringer of potions that transformed and transported them, and made Thora's marital woes vanish like demons fleeing an exorcist's prayer. He was all of these and more. Sex with Thora placed him behind many masks on many occasions. But at none of these times had he lost his ability to distinguish fact from fallacy. Despite all the states of being that their dalliances had thrust upon him, Thora would never be his.

*****

"So are we doing this or what? Why are you still dressed?" Thora asked Alton, shedding clothes around his bedroom floor like a molting serpent wriggling free of skin it has outgrown. As always, contemplation of her wholly unobstructed nakedness was nearly more than Alton could bear to gaze upon. As always, he found himself reminded that Horace was a dipshit.

Thora hadn't simply come to Alton for sex. Thora *was* sex; shaven, lustrous, pagan goddess sex that knew his name and spoke it like a prayer when his tongue inscribed his petitions upon her clitoris. Thora was feral, breakneck sex with legs composing the lion's share of a five foot eleven inch climb that rewarded and exhausted beyond the ken of the most seasoned mountaineer's experiences. She was a solar eclipse, a breathing aphrodisiac upon which he could not long look without collapsing beneath the weight of his depravities. A woman of such perfect lewdness and boundless imagination as to render her incapable of being soiled was a rarity unparalleled.

"So get in bed," Alton said, unbuttoning his jeans, letting gravity guide them down his legs like a lover. He stepped out of them to reveal that his habit of forgoing underwear when at home was intact. His tee shirt tore away from his body and leapt from sight and mind as he tossed it away and started toward her. Thora retreated, her breasts bobbling as she hopped smirking beyond his grasp, her gaze stroking the fruit ripening between his thighs in a way that Alton could almost feel.

"Bring the Beam," Thora told him, lifting her emptied glass, "I could stand another hit, and so could you." As she spoke, she dragged the lightweight coverlet and top sheet off his bed and onto the floor. There was a viscosity to the way she moved that made an obscenity of the act, as if the air surrounding them was an ocean through which she swam envied by every living thing. Cast down bed coverings spread over the floor at the foot of Alton's king-size bed, tides rolling in at Thora's behest to meet the faux-wood shores of a forgotten beach where none should ever find them.

"One's enough for me, but I'll bring it for you," Alton's chief reason for keeping the stuff in his kitchen was that Thora liked it, but rarely did he drink it himself unless she was visiting. As his taste in spirits went, vodka was the poison he'd chosen at age seventeen and to which he remained devoted to this day. On those rare occasions when the fancy for deviation from the familiar took him, his preferred method of savoring was to bind Thora's ankles to the spreader bar he kept beneath his bed, and lap the spirit of choice with aching slowness from Thora's toes, whose sensitivity to tickling was surpassed only by that of her bare ribs. Tonight, however, no such wanderlust gripped his palate, and so Alton would, for the moment, forgo a second drink.

"Candy ass," Thora derided, stalking onto his unmade bed, a tawny lioness in heat.

"We'll see," Alton said, leaving to retrieve the bottle of Jim Beam. Horace, like the wife he neglected, was a hard one to pity, given the circumstances that had not only made him wealthy, but paired him with a woman fifteen years his junior, the limits of whose unchained libido Alton had not yet witnessed. Her being eight years Alton's senior notwithstanding, it had become all that he could do to keep pace with her when Thora's need to punish Horace's professional preoccupation found them naked together with Alton filling her.

He returned to the bedroom to find Thora lounging, comfortably draped over two of his bed pillows that she'd stacked upon one another. Her sex she'd raised in undeniable invitation to begin their festival of flesh. Her glass rested between her fingertips. She extended it in her right hand, and Alton added two fingers' worth of Beam.

"Ice?" she asked.

"I thought ice was for pansies," Alton replied.

"That only goes for men," Thora said in a tone that did not require her to conclude her sentence with the word "idiot" to drive the sentiment deep into Alton's chest.

"You didn't take ice the first time." He countered, unbothered by the barb, but toying with her sheerly out of amused spite.

"I could spend the rest of the day explaining a woman's prerogatives to you," Thora told him, "but that's time better spent by you throwing some rocks where I need them." She shook her glass again and smiled with a warmth suggesting there was a joke they were both in on, and that perhaps some form of foreplay existed between them after all. Alton made a dramatic performance of pretending to sigh and loped out to the kitchen with his head hanging. He returned a moment later.

"Here's your goddamned ice," Alton said, pushing the glass into Thora's hands.

Alton took his place in bed with Thora like a peasant invited into royal court. For the next couple of hours, they would revel in comforting illusions of being more to each other than they were or would ever be. It seemed to him, a crime unspeakable that naked, in the most candid, exposed state attainable by human beings, each of them was the other's greatest fable ever told. Him, a surgeon when it came to getting her off with precision, everything between the sheets and between the legs that Horace could never be, poor bastard. Her, that woman that lived in every man's imagination, the one so far beyond his league of the attainable that the idea of her interest in him is a bad joke, who yet inexplicably finds her way into his bed. Laying with her was the calm before the storm, and tonight, Alton was the storm she'd be riding.

"Now then," Thora smiled, swallowing the remainder of the refreshed drink he'd iced for her, and clasping her moist, cool hand around his stiffness, "Let's get this wet."

Thora climbed astride his shoulders, her nether lips bestowing their ethereal kiss upon his mouth, her hair a dark shroud through which he always expected to see stars shooting. Her arousal musk wafted.

Alton stiffened as her lips descended his glans and pushed low, packing his helmet into her throat. Time evaporated in the heat of her tongue, a water droplet dancing upon a fired skillet. Thora's brown buttocks tensed as his tongue probed her crevice. Alton sucked earthquakes from her clitoris, sent them rolling along her frame and into open air on the wings of her cries and moans. Alton soon lost himself inside her mouth. By the time they rolled over for her to fold those impossibly long legs around him, Alton felt as through stars were shooting through him.

Brown breasts pushed into his hands. Alton felt as always, like a thief in a hallowed temple. Stabbing himself deep into her garden of roses, he snarled at her tightness. Thora snarled back as she hurled her pelvis at him, daring him to make good on the feral promises his eyes licked into her skin. On his knees and stomach, on his side, and on his back, Alton made good on every one.

*****

Alton awoke sometime later to find the sun and moon sharing the sky beyond his bedroom window. Like disapproving eyes. Admonishing him.

"Did you enjoy yourself?" Thora's tone kept no secrets. It did not endeavor to conceal her question's rhetorical nature, nor of the importance of Alton's answer pleasing her.

"Always do," he sighed honestly. Beyond his bedroom, gathering winds whispered black things that questioned Alton's wisdom. Thora might well be the most beauteous woman and best fuck ever to grace his humble bed, but she was no less married for it. That he'd shared as many orgasms with her as he had bordered on the miraculous. How far he could press his good fortune before having to answer for his actions was a thing none except Horace could say. The man was certain to discover his wife's infidelity soon enough, if he was not already onto her.

Although Alton felt confident that if Thora's husband came calling with a mad on for him, he could kick the shit out of the old fart, such a confrontation was nothing to which Alton aspired.

"Good," Thora told him simply. She would offer him no such reassurance as she'd sought, and Alton knew better than to request any. The savagery of her orgasms was always sufficient proof that she'd had as good a time as he.

Something struck the side of his house hard. Something that sounded big and had stuck with force enough to rattle the wall-mounted bookshelves above Alton's bed.

"What the hell was that?" Alton shrieked at a pitch that immediately embarrassed him.

Another thud followed, this one sounding beyond the bedroom, against the outer face of Alton's living room wall. Alton heard glass shatter.

"Sounds to me like the end of the road," Thora sighed, sounding sullen and despondent.

"This is serious," he told Thora, "What the fuck's going on? Are we under some kind of attack?"

"You have eyes. And feet," Thora told him, stretching seductively upon his sheets. Her disinterest was palpable.

Alton swore, got to his feet and leapt from bed to peer out his bedroom window. Before he went charging into the living room he damned well needed to know what he was getting himself into.

Another impact slammed against the house, its force veining Alton's bedroom window. Another followed. Upon his roof, something scratched and scraped with the tenacity of a burglar knowing that beyond that barrier, treasure awaited.

Barely visible was the dusk sky beyond Alton's window, so numerous were the hovering judges that populated it. Thousands of keen eyes glared back at Alton through that window where falcons of every stripe stood like grim sentries occupying the grounds surrounding his home, perched upon his car, upon the fences between his yard and his neighbor's. Deafening the sound of thousands of falcons' wings beating a death knell into the air where they hovered. For as far to the left and right as he could look without opening the window to lean out, the creatures clamored.

Alton had never seen so many of the birds in one place, nor had he ever seen such large ones as apparently had come to deliver their message. They looked nearly as tall as Alton himself.

"Thora, for God's sake!" Alton begged, not comprehending how or why she could be so goddamned calm. Another series of hard impacts against the house shook Alton, nearly startling him off his feet.

In the living room, glass continued to break. The sound of the raptors divebombing his residence was constant and terrifying enough to drag Alton ever closer to screaming.

"Ignore them," Thora insisted, "They're my husband's messengers. But I have no patience for his dramatics, or yours.

Now, pour me a drink and we'll see about another roll in the hay before–"

"Damn it, wait a minute," Alton interrupted, "What are you talking about? Horace is doing this? How the hell can this be Horace's doing?"

"Not 'Horace,'" said the impossibly deep male voice that sounded behind him, "*Horus*."

Alton's testicles disappeared up into his body. He turned to find his bedroom doorway filled with a male figure whose impressive brown musculature glistened with light from an unexplained source. The intruder, naked but for a loin shroud of woven gold, stood over eight feet tall, his chiseled physique betraying not an ounce of fat. At such height and girth, he had to weigh several hundred pounds.

Jeweled bands adorned the stranger's ankles, ringed his arms, which were easily thicker than Alton's thighs, just above those massive biceps. Most frightening of all was that the towering presence that had forced its way into Alton's home to challenge him where he stood naked and impotent before it, bore the head of a glaring falcon.

Horus, Alton thought, as sanity left him, *Egyptian falcon god Horus. . .*

"Husband," Thora smirked. Alton wondered why this one time in his life that he would have welcomed fainting dead away, he seemed unable to grant himself such mercy.

"Wife. Are we here again?," Horus replied in a baritone as dead as Alton imagined he himself would soon be. Surely only a person so foolhardy as to have tired of living would risk angering a behemoth the likes of the one whose bare feet stood burning footprints the size of welcome mats into Alton's carpet.

Alton's thoughts raced. *Egyptian* war *god Horus*, they sang, *and I just finished fucking his wife. . .*

“Leave me, *Heru*. Let me enjoy my distraction,” Thora told the giant, leaving the bed to come stand beside Alton and tousle his head as though he were an adorable child.

“Hathor, or should I call you ‘Sehmet?’” Horus bellowed, “Stand down. Now. “

“You surprise me, husband,” Thora said, “Always telling *me* to keep a low profile? Low profile indeed. . .”

“Delight though you may, in these. . .diversions, your place is with your husband. Come home with me,” Horus demanded.

“These ‘diversions’ are all that is left to me, Heru,” Thora told him, “You’d rather spend your time basking in the adoration of your human worshippers than that of your soulmate. Do not be angry simply because I’ve come around to your way of thinking.”

Horus replied, “My responsibilities toward the inhabitants of this world are well known to you. There was a time when you remembered that you have responsibilities of your own. You will come home and sleep. You’ll feel better when you awaken. Then, we can discuss this further.”

The words would suffer no argument. Hathor’s scattered clothing vanished from the places around Alton’s apartment where she’d cast them. A dress of shimmering jewels and woven gold fabric materialized on her. She was beyond exquisite.

“It’s been fun,” Hathor told Alton, sounding sincere, “I’ll miss venting to you. But we knew what this was from the beginning, right?”

To Alton, the dark-skinned visitor said, “In the future, you would do well to take more care with what married women you bring to your bed.”

Alton could not move, too terrified that he would incite the god defying reality in his doorway. Alton could not speak, the events transpiring around him too far beyond his understanding for him to have any idea what to say, or to whom to say it first. He promised himself that he would never again sleep with another man's wife.

Horus' thoughts touched Alton's. *No*, they assured him, *you most certainly will not*.

Hathor smiled at Alton in a way that, despite his fear of Horus, momentarily revived his lust and made him feel lucky for having enjoyed multiple expeditions inside her. "Goodbye, Alton. I will long remember your skill at taking me away from things at home that I could suffer no longer."

"See that his promise is kept," Horus commanded his charges, indicating Alton with a disgusted glance as he and his wife turned and departed. Horus transformed into a flurry of winging falcons that surrounded Thora and vanished with her, carrying her back to where goddesses belonged .

The last thing that Alton would ever see was scores of man-sized falcons with beaks like scalpels pouring into his bedroom through the window, stalking onto his bed like restitution-seeking lovers done wrong, flooding in from his living room shrieking damning admonishments, coming to ensure that he did indeed keep his promise.

About the Author:

NY native Anthony Beal enjoys writing, wines, and cooking spicy food. He has published in over one hundred print and online publications, and collects books and music like they've been outlawed.

His other interests include anime, Food Network programming, graphic novels, studying the Japanese language, the poetry of Paul Lawrence Dunbar, the fiction of Gabriel Garcia Marquez, and web authoring.

His writing is influenced by Marquez and Dunbar, as well as by Poe, Brite, Equiano, and Lovecraft. He enjoys authoring and maintaining his official web presence at www.TheOfficialAnthonyBeal.com, where he regularly posts excerpts of his dark erotica.

Other Works by Anthony Beal:

Naked, Shamed With Their Pleasures, They Wept: 52 Erotic Verses

This Gift of Black Roses: Thirteen Horror Tales for Reading by Candlelight

Previously published works appearing in this collection:

"**Fidem Meam Noto**" first published in anthology BE MINE *(edited by L. Marie Wood)*, February 2004

"**Lord of All That Glitters**" first published in anthology *DARK DREAMS II (edited by Brandon Massey)*, February 2005

"**Reliquary**" first published in *Lucrezia Magazine*, March 2009

"**Saving Evan**" first published in *Niteblade Fantasy and Horror Magazine*, March 2008

"**Shadow Girl**" first published in *Shadow of the Marquis*, February 2003

"**The Gift of Infinite Midnight**" first published in anthology *VINTAGE MOON - Tales of Vampires and Werewolves (edited by Nancy Jackson)*, October 2006

Cover Image Source Credit:

"Red rose of skull and bones" copyright © 2008 -
Vector created by iStockPhoto Member *Polygraphus,* Silver Contributor

www.ingramcontent.com/pod-product-compliance
Lightning Source LLC
LaVergne TN
LVHW091000080826
845145LV00003B/1067

* 9 7 8 0 5 7 8 0 2 2 1 2 3 *